"I cannot think why you persist in annoying me, Professor van Rakesma."

"I am not sure myself," he told Mary mildly. "You are a perpetual thorn in my otherwise disciplined life." He turned to look at her. "To mix my metaphors, you are like a sore tooth that I'm unable to leave alone."

Her brown eyes flashed with temper. "Well, a thorn, indeed, a sore tooth—whatever next, I should like to know?"

"I've been wondering that myself. Do you suppose we might cry quits and become friends?"

Friends, thought Mary wildly. Who wants to be friends? And he's almost a married man.

"Certainly not."

"You don't like me?"

"I didn't say that."

"Good, in that case let us at least assume an armed neutrality."

Betty Neels spent her childhood and youth in Devonshire, England before training as a nurse and midwife. She was an army nursing sister during the war, married a Dutchman and subsequently lived in Holland for fourteen years. She lives with her husband in Dorset, and has a daughter and grandson. Her hobbies are reading, animals, old buildings and writing. Betty started to write on retirement from nursing, incited by a lady in a library bemoaning the lack of romantic novels.

Books by Betty Neels

HARLEQUIN ROMANCE
3415—THE BACHELOR'S WEDDING
3454—FATE TAKES A HAND
3467—THE RIGHT KIND OF GIRL
3483—THE MISTLETOE KISS

Don't miss any of our special offers. Write to us at the following address for information on our newest releases.

Harlequin Reader Service
U.S.: 3010 Walden Ave., P.O. Box 1325, Buffalo, NY 14269
Canadian: P.O. Box 609, Fort Erie, Ont. L2A 5X3

Betty Neels
Marrying Mary

Harlequin Books

TORONTO • NEW YORK • LONDON
AMSTERDAM • PARIS • SYDNEY • HAMBURG
STOCKHOLM • ATHENS • TOKYO • MILAN
MADRID • WARSAW • BUDAPEST • AUCKLAND

ISBN 0-373-03492-X

MARRYING MARY

First North American Publication 1998.

Copyright © 1996 by Betty Neels.

This edition published by arrangement with Harlequin Books S.A.

® and TM are trademarks of the publisher. Trademarks indicated with ® are registered in the United States Patent and Trademark Office, the Canadian Trade Marks Office and in other countries.

Printed in U.S.A.

CHAPTER ONE

MARY PAGETT, stripping a bed with energy, was singing at the top of her voice. Not because she was happy, but to quell the frustration within. For her father—that charming but absent-minded man—to invite Great Aunt Thirza to spend her convalescence at his home had been a misplaced kindness, bringing with it a string of inconveniences which would have to be overcome.

For a start Mrs Blackett, who came daily to oblige and suffered from a persistent ill temper, was going to object to peeling more potatoes and scraping more carrots, not to mention the extra work vacuuming the guest bedroom. And Mr Archer, the village butcher, was going to express hurt feelings at the lack of orders for sausages and braising steak, since Great Aunt Thirza was a vegetarian, and for reasons of economy the rest of the household would have to be vegetarian too.

There was her mother too—Mary's voice rose a few decibels—a lovable, whimsical lady, whose talent for designing Christmas cards had earned her a hut in the garden to which she retired after breakfast each day, only appearing at meals. Lastly there was Polly, her young sister, who was a keen and not very accurate player of the recorder; her loving family bore with the noise but Great Aunt Thirza was going to object ...

Mary finished making the bed, cast an eye over the rather heavy furniture in the high-ceilinged room, with its old-fashioned wallpaper and wooden floor, sparsely covered by elderly rugs, and hoped that the draughts

from the big sash windows opposite wouldn't be too
much for her elderly relation.

The house—a mid-Victorian rectory built for an in-
cumbent with a large family—wasn't all that old. After
standing empty for some years it had been bought by
her father, since it had been a bargain at its low price.
But he, an unworldly man, had not taken notice of the
size of its rooms, which made heating the place almost
hopeless, or the lack of maids, or the fact that coal for
the enormous grates was a constant drain on the
household purse—nor had he considered the amount of
gas and electricity which was needed.

He had his study, where he worked on his book, and
Mary's pleas for someone to clear the drains, paint the
doors and put tiles back on the elaborate roof fell on
deaf ears.

Her father was a dear man, she reflected, but unworldly. He was devoted to his wife and children, but
that had never prevented him from delegating the
mundane responsibilities of a married man to someone
else and, since Mary was so conveniently there, they had
fallen to her.

It had happened very gradually; she had left school
with hopes of going on to university, but her mother had
been ill and her two brothers had been home, and
someone had had to feed and look after them—besides
which Polly had still been a little girl. Her mother had
got better, the boys had gone to Cambridge, but no one
had suggested that Mary might like to do anything but
stay home and look after them all. She had stayed quite
willingly since, despite its drawbacks, she loved the
shabby old house, she liked cooking, and she even liked
a certain amount of housework.

So the years had slipped quietly by, and here she was, twenty-four years old, a tall, splendidly built girl with a lovely face, enormous brown eyes and an abundance of chestnut hair, her face rendered even more interesting by reason of her nose, which was short and tip-tilted. It went without saying that the men of her acquaintance liked her, admired her and in two cases had wished to marry her. She had refused them kindly and remained firm friends, acting as bridesmaid at their weddings and godmother to their children.

There was Arthur, of course, whom she had known for years—a worthy young man who rather took it for granted that one day she would marry him, and indeed from time to time she had considered that possibility. He would be a splendid husband—faithful and kind even if a bit bossy. He was also a shade pompous and she had doubts as to what he would be like in ten years' time.

Besides, she had no intention of marrying anyone at the moment; the boys were away from home but Polly was thirteen—too young to be left to the care of a fond but unworldly mother and a forgetful father. Right at the back of her head was the half-formed wish that something exciting would happen—something so exciting and urgent that her prosaic plans would be dashed to pieces...

The only thing that was going to happen was Great Aunt Thirza, who was neither of these things, but a cantankerous old lady who liked her own way.

Mary went down to the kitchen and broke the news to Mrs Blackett, who paused long enough in her cleaning of the kitchen floor with far too wet a mop to scowl at her and grumble with such venom that her dentures got dislodged.

'As though we 'aven't got enough on our 'ands. And it's no good you expecting me to do more for you than what I do now.' She gave a snort of ill humour and sloshed more water over the floor.

Mary, side-stepping the puddles, made soothing noises. 'When you've finished the floor,' she said cheerfully, 'we'll have a cup of tea. I wouldn't expect you to do more than you do already, Mrs Blackett, and I dare say that Great Aunt Thirza will spend a good deal of time resting.'

Knowing that lady, she thought it unlikely, but Mrs Blackett wasn't to know that, and the latter, calmed with a strong cup of tea and a large slice of cake, relating the latest misdemeanour of Horace, her youngest, became sufficiently mollified to suggest doing a bit extra around the house. 'I'd stay for me dinner and do a couple of hours in an afternoon—it'd 'ave to be a Tuesday or a Wednesday, mind.'

Mary accepted her offer gratefully. 'It will only be for a week or two, Mrs Blackett.'

'Where's she coming from, then?'

'She's in St Justin's. Her housekeeper will take whatever clothes she needs to the hospital and an ambulance will bring her here.' Mary gave a very small sigh. 'Tomorrow.'

'You'll want more spuds,' said Mrs Blackett. 'Going ter get a nice bit of 'am?'

'Well, I'm afraid that Mrs Winton is a vegetarian...'

'I don't 'old with them,' said Mrs Blackett darkly.

Nor did Mary, although she sympathised with their views.

She took a basket from the hook behind the kitchen door and went down the garden to pick beans, pull new carrots and cut spinach. Thank heaven it was early summer and her small kitchen garden was flourishing, although she would have to go to the greengrocer presently and get more vegetables, as well as beans and lentils and spaghetti. She hoped that Great Aunt Thirza would like that, though she was doubtful if anyone else would.

Before going back into the house she stopped to look around her. The house was on the edge of Hampstead Heath, with Golders Green not far away, and the garden offered a pleasant view and she stood admiring it. It would be nice to spend a day in the country, she reflected, and thought of her childhood, spent in a rambling cottage in Gloucestershire.

They might still be there but for the fact that her father had needed to be nearer the British Museum so that he could do his research and her mother had wanted a closer contact with the agent who sold her cards. Polly hadn't been born then, and although it hadn't mattered much to the boys, who had been at boarding-school anyway, Mary had taken some time to settle down at her new school and make new friends.

She went back indoors and presently out to the butcher, where, since it was likely to be the last meat they would have for a while, she bought steak and kidney in a generous amount and bore it home. It was a warm day for steak and kidney pudding but she was rewarded that evening by the pleasure with which it was received.

'Everything all right, dear?' asked her mother, and before she could reply added, 'I've had a letter from Mr Thorne—the agent—he's got me a splendid commission. I shall have to work at it, though—you'll be quite happy with Great Aunt Thirza?'

Mary assured her that she would. She wasn't surprised to hear from her father that he would be away

all day at the British Museum. 'But I'll be home in time
to welcome Thirza,' he said. 'Make her comfortable,
won't you, my dear?'

'I'll play her "Greensleeves",' offered Polly.

'That'll be lovely, darling,' said Mrs Pagett. 'It's so
nice that you're musical.'

Mrs Winton arrived the next day in nice time for tea.
She was tall and thin with a high-bridged nose, upon
which rested her pince-nez, and she wore a beautifully
cut coat and skirt of the style fashionable in the early
decades of the century, and crowned this with a wide-
brimmed straw hat. She had the same kind of hat, only
in felt, during the winter months.

Mary had gone to the door to meet her and watched
while the ambulancemen settled her into a chair and
trundled her over.

'That will do, thank you,' said Great Aunt Thirza.
'My niece will help me into the sitting-room.' She turned
to look at her. 'Well, Mary, here I am.'

Mary kissed the offered cheek. 'We are delighted to
have you to stay, Aunt.' She stopped as the men turned
away. 'If you'd like to go to the kitchen—the door over
there—there's tea and sandwiches. Thank you both so
much.'

She had a lovely smile and they beamed back at her.
'If that's not troubling you, miss, we could do with a
cuppa.'

'Would you like tea, Aunt Thirza? It's all ready in the
sitting-room.' She gave the old lady an arm and settled
her in an armchair by the small tea-table. 'Father's at
the British Museum; he'll be back at any moment.
Mother's very busy; she's just had an order for
Christmas cards.'

'Ridiculous,' said Mrs Winton. 'Christmas cards, indeed—child's play.'

'Actually they need a great deal of skill, and Mother's very good at them.'

Her aunt sipped her tea. 'Why aren't you married, Mary?'

'Well, I don't think I've met anyone I want to marry yet. There's Arthur, of course...'

'A girl should marry.' She pronounced it 'gel'. 'I don't hold with this independence. My generation had more sense; we married and settled down to be good wives and mothers.'

Aunt Thirza was in her eighties. Mary wondered what it had been like to be young then—corsets and hats and gloves, not just on Sundays and occasions but even to go shopping, and not to be able to drive a car or wear trousers...

On the other hand there had been no television and there had been dances—not the leaping around that was the fashion now, but foxtrotting and waltzing. Waltzing with a man you loved or even liked must have been delightful. The clothes had been pretty awful, but they were pretty awful nowadays among the young. Mary, who sometimes felt older than her years, sighed.

Great Aunt Thirza was quite a handful. She had brought a good deal of luggage with her which had to be unpacked and disposed around the house according to her fancy. She poked her nose into the kitchen and made scathing remarks about Mrs Blackett's terrible old slippers with the nicks cut out for the comfort of her bunions; she inspected the fridge, lectured Polly on her untidiness, interrupted her nephew in his study and swept down to the hut to see her niece-in-law, where she passed so many critical remarks that that lady was unable to pick up her brush for the rest of the day.

It didn't matter how ingenious Mary was with the lentils, dried peas and beans, her elderly relation always found something wrong with them.

At the end of a week, having escorted her to her room, shut the windows, refreshed the water jug, gone down-stairs again for warm milk, found another blanket, run a bath and listened to her aunt giving her opinion of the drawbacks of the house, Mary went downstairs to where her mother and father were sitting in the drawing-room— a room seldom used since it was large, draughty and, despite Mary's polishing, shabby.

'When is Great Aunt Thirza going home?' she asked her father, sounding cross.

He looked up from the book he was reading, peered over his glasses at her and said mildly, 'I really don't know, my dear. She's no trouble, is she?'

Mary sat down. 'Yes, Father, she is. She has made Mrs Blackett even more bad-tempered than usual—she's threatened to leave—and Polly is rebellious and I can't blame her. I haven't cooked a square meal for more than a week; I don't expect that you've noticed but there's not been an ounce of meat in the house for days and I, for one, am sick of spinach and lettuce leaves.'

Her mother looked up from the sketches she was making. 'A nice steak with mushrooms, and those French fries you do so well, darling.' She added hopefully, 'Could we go out for a meal?'

'It would cost too much,' said Mary, who knew more about the housekeeping money than her mother. 'We need a miracle...'

*   *   *

It came with the postman in the morning. Great Aunt Thirza was bidden to attend at St Justin's in Central London where she had been treated for a heart condition—nine o'clock on the following morning. Should her examination prove satisfactory she could make arrangements to return to her home and resume a normal life.

'I shall, of course, abide by the specialist's advice,' said Great Aunt Thirza. 'He may consider it more beneficial to my health for me to return here for a further few weeks.' She poured herself another cup of tea—the special herbal one that she preferred. 'You can drive me there, Mary. It will save the expense of a taxi.'

Mary didn't answer. Mrs Winton was comfortably off, well able to afford as many taxis as she could want; she could afford to pay for the peas and beans too, thought Mary peevishly.

To waste most of a day, certainly a whole morning, taking her aunt to the hospital was tiresome when there was a stack of ironing waiting to be done, besides which she needed to thumb through the cookery book she had borrowed from the library and find another way to cook kidney beans...

Polly, back from school at teatime, gobbling bread spread with an imitation butter, heavily covered with peanut butter, voiced the opinion that Great Aunt Thirza was quite well enough to go home. 'Let her housekeeper cook that rabbit food.' She rolled her large blue eyes dramatically. 'Mary, I'll die if I don't have some chips soon.'

'Perhaps I could have a word with the specialist,' mused Mary.

'Yes, do. Wear something pretty and flutter your eyelashes at him. You're quite pretty, you know.'

'I don't expect that kind of man—you know, wildly clever and always reading books like Father, only younger—notices if one is pretty or not. If I had a heart attack or fainted all over him he might, I suppose.'

She spent a moment imagining herself falling gracefully into the arms of some doddering old professor. It wouldn't do; she wasn't the right shape. Fainting was for small, ethereal girls with tiny waists and slender enough to be picked up easily. Whoever it was who caught her would need to be a giant with muscles to match. 'But I will wear that green dress and those sandals I bought in the sales.'

St Justin's Hospital wasn't far as the crow flew, but driving there during the rush hour was a different matter. Great Aunt Thirza, roused from her bed at an early hour, was in a bad temper. She sat beside Mary, her lips firmly closed, wearing the air of someone who was being shabbily treated but refused to complain, which left Mary free to concentrate on getting to the hospital by nine o'clock.

The outpatients department was already full. They were told where to sit and warned that Mr van Rakesma had not yet arrived but was expected at any moment. 'I am probably the first to be seen,' said Great Aunt Thirza. She edged away from an elderly man beside her who was asleep and snoring gently. 'Really, the people one meets; I find it distasteful.'

'You could always be a private patient,' suggested Mary.

'My dear Mary, you talk as though I had a fortune. Besides, why should I pay for something I can obtain for nothing?'

Mary wondered if having money made one mean. She wasn't interested in her aunt's finances. She changed places with the old lady and found that the snoring man was watching her. 'Morning, love,' he said cheerfully. 'Don't tell me someone as pretty as you needs to come to this halfway house.'

'Halfway house?'

He winked. 'Take a look, love. We're all getting a bit long in the tooth and needing a bit of make do and mend to help us on our way!' He winked again and added, 'Who's the old biddy with you? Not your ma, that's for sure.'

'An aunt—a great aunt actually. Shall we have to wait for a long time?'

He waved a vague arm. 'Starts at eight o'clock, does his nibs, but, seeing that he's not here yet and it's gone nine o'clock, I'd say we'll still be here for our dinner.'

'You mean the first appointment is for eight o'clock?' When he nodded she said, 'My aunt thought she would be the first patient.'

His loud laugh caused Great Aunt Thirza to bend forward and look around Mary so that she could give him an icy stare.

'I cannot imagine why this man hasn't come, Mary. Possibly he is still in his bed...'

He wasn't, though. There was a wave of interest in the closely packed benches as he walked past them—a very tall, heavily built man, his gingery hair tinged with grey, his handsome face without expression, looking ahead of him just as though there was no one else there but himself and his registrar beside him. Mary had ample opportunity to study him. He was, she realised, the man she had been waiting for, and she fell instantly in love with him.

After that she didn't mind the long wait, and sat between the now sleeping man and an irate great aunt. She had plenty to think about, and most of her thoughts were of a highly impractical nature, but just for the moment she allowed day-dreaming to override common sense. He would look at her and fall in love, just as she had done...

'At last,' hissed Great Aunt Thirza. 'Come with me, Mary.'

The consulting-room was quite small and Mr van Rakesma seemed to take up most of it. He glanced up briefly as they went in, asked them to sit down in a pleasant, impersonal voice and finished his writing.

'Mrs Winton? You have been referred to me by Dr Cymes and I am glad to see you looking so well.' He glanced at the notes before him. 'You wish to return home, I understand, and if I find you quite recovered I see no reason why you shouldn't do so.'

'Young man,' said Great Aunt Thirza sternly, 'I had an appointment for nine o'clock this morning. It is now ten minutes past twelve. I consider this a disgraceful state of affairs.'

Mary went pink and stared at her feet. Mr van Rakesma smiled; Sister, standing beside his desk, gave an indignant snort.

'Circumstances occasionally arise which prevent our keeping to our original plans,' he said mildly. 'Would you be good enough to go with Sister to the examination-room so that I can take a look?'

'You will stay here,' she told Mary as she went. Mary didn't look up, which was a pity for she would have found his eyes on her. He couldn't see her face, but her glorious hair was enough to attract any man's eye...

'Is there something wrong with your shoe?' he asked gently.

She looked at him then, still pink. 'No—no.' She went on rapidly, 'My aunt's tired; she didn't mean what she said.'

He smiled and her heart danced against her ribs. 'No? A disappointment; I rather liked being called "young man".' He got up and went into the examination-room, and when he came out again presently he didn't so much as glance at her but sat down and began to write. When Mrs Winton reappeared he told her that for her age she was very fit and there was no reason why she shouldn't resume a normal lifestyle.

'You have someone to look after you? A housekeeper? A daughter?'

'A housekeeper and, of course, should I require extra help, my niece——' she nodded at Mary '—would come.'

He nodded. 'Then everything seems most satisfactory, Mrs Winton.' He stood up and shook hands with her and bade her a grave goodbye, gave Mary a brief, unsmiling nod, then sat down and took up his pen once more.

It was Sister who said, 'You'll need an appointment for six months' time, Mrs Winton; go and see Reception as you go out. Professor van Rakesma will want to keep an eye on you.'

Great Aunt Thirza stopped short. 'Professor? You mean to tell me that he's a professor?'

'Yes, and a very clever one too, Mrs Winton. We're lucky to have him for a consultant.'

Over lunch at a nearby café, Great Aunt Thirza observed that for a foreigner his manners had been surprisingly good. Mary murmured a reply, busy with her own thoughts.

'Presumably,' went on Great Aunt Thirza, 'he is reliable.'

'Well, he's a professor. I expect he had to take exams or something before he could be one.'

'I trust the exams were taken here in England. Our standards are high.'

'Wasn't the seat of medical learning Leiden? I believe it is still considered one of the best medical schools...' She added, 'He is Dutch.'

'That is as may be,' observed the old lady. 'I shall check with Dr Cymes.'

Mary, who had been wondering how she could find out more about the professor, said casually, 'What a good idea. You must let me know what he says. Probably he's over here on some exchange scheme.'

It was a slender chance, she thought wistfully; it was unlikely that she would ever see him again. How silly she was to fall in love with a complete stranger. 'We'd better start back,' she said briskly. 'You'll want to ring your housekeeper and arrange things.'

'Naturally. I intend to leave your father's house in two days' time; that will give us the opportunity to pack my things. You will, of course, drive me home.'

At the thought of eating sausages and the weekend joint again Mary sighed with relief; she would have driven her great aunt to the furthest corner of the land...

Her mother and father expressed pleasure at Mrs Winton's recovery, and pressed her to stay as long as she wished, unaware of Mary's speaking glance. Mary could see her wavering. Something had to be done—and quickly. 'Polly, fetch your recorder and play something for Great Aunt Thirza.'

A wobbly rendering of 'Greensleeves', followed by an unrecognisable piece full of wrong notes, which Polly

assured them was 'The Trout' by Schubert, put an end
to the old lady's indecision; she would return home, as
she had first intended, in two days' time.

It fell to Mary's lot, naturally enough, to pack for her
aunt, and then unpack everything again because that lady
suddenly remembered that she would need a particular
cardigan to wear. She did it all cheerfully, quite un-
moved by her aunt's fault-finding and lack of thanks,
and two days later she got the car out, loaded the cases
and settled Mrs Winton on the back seat.

Her father had come out of his study to say goodbye
and her mother, in her painting smock and holding a
brush in her hand, had joined him on the doorstep. Polly
wasn't back from school but Mrs Blackett, obliging with
an extra afternoon's work, glowered from the kitchen
window.

Great Aunt Thirza said her goodbyes graciously,
omitting to thank anyone, giving the impression that she
had honoured them greatly by her visit and pausing long
enough in the hall to find fault with several things around
the house. 'I'm sure, though, that you did your best,'
she added, 'and on the whole the meals were palatable.'

These remarks were met in silence. 'I dare say I shall
see improvements when I next visit you,' she said and
swept out to the car.

The Pagetts watched their daughter drive away.
'Perhaps we should wait a little before we invite dear
Aunt Thirza to stay again, my dear,' observed Mr Pagett,
and added, 'I do hope Mary will cook something tasty
for supper...'

Mrs Winton lived in Richmond in a red-brick terraced
house, which was much too large for her and stuffed
with mid-Victorian furniture, heavy plush curtains and
a great many ornaments. Her housekeeper had been with

her for a good number of years—a silent, austere woman
who kept her distance, ran the house efficiently and never
talked about herself, which wasn't surprising really since
Mrs Winton never asked.

She opened the door as Mary stopped the car, wished
them good afternoon and took Mrs Winton's luggage
from the boot. 'We'd like tea at once, Mrs Cox,' said
Great Aunt Thirza, and swept indoors with a brisk,
'Come along, Mary; don't dawdle!'

Mary wasn't listening; she had gone back to the car
to give Mrs Cox a hand with the luggage.

She hadn't wanted to stay for tea but good manners
made it necessary; she sat on an uncomfortable horsehair
chair—a museum piece if ever there was one—and drank
weak tea from a beautiful Minton cup and ate a dry
Madeira cake which she suspected had been in the tin
ever since Great Aunt Thirza's illness.

While she ate she thought of the sausages and the
mountains of chips she would cook when she got home.
She had no doubt that her mother and father and Polly
would enjoy them as much as she would.

Driving back presently, it wasn't sausages and chips
on her mind, it was love—the sheer excitement of it, the
wonder of it, just to look at someone and know that he
was the one... Her euphoria was short-lived. 'Fool,' said
Mary. 'You'll never see him again—it was pure chance;
besides, he didn't even look at you.'

She edged past a slow-moving Ford Anglia, driven by
an elderly man in a cloth cap. 'He'll be married to some
gorgeous wisp of a girl who he'll treat like fragile porcelain.' She sighed; no one, however kindly disposed,
could describe her as fragile. 'All the same, it would be
nice to find out about him.'

She was talking to herself again, waiting at traffic lights, and the driver of the car alongside hers gave her a startled look. She looked sane enough, but he couldn't see anyone else in the car...

Professor van Rakesma, unlike Mary, wasn't talking to himself—he was going through the notes of his patients.

'Mrs Winton,' he said at length in a satisfied voice, and made a note of her address. He had no doubt at all that he would discover more of the girl who had been with her—a niece, the old lady had said, and one in the habit of giving extra help and therefore to be tracked down at some future date.

He handed the notes back to the patient nurse waiting for them and left the hospital. He was dining out with friends and anticipating a pleasant evening as well as an excellent dinner.

Mary and her family had an excellent dinner too; the sausages and chips were greeted with whoops of joy from Polly, and even her mother, a dainty eater, welcomed them with pleasure. There was a wholesome roly-poly pudding for afters too, and a bottle of red wine, pronounced delicious by everyone.

Her father, of course, hardly noticed what he drank, and her mother was too kind to do more than remark on its good colour. The professor, had he been there, would have poured it down the sink.

Never mind that—it was a celebration; they were a family again without Great Aunt Thirza to meddle and complain. No one actually said that; only Polly remarked that she hoped that her great aunt wouldn't pay them another visit for a very long time.

'Well, she only comes when she wants something,' said Polly, 'and she's well again now isn't she?'

'She saw a specialist the other day?' asked her mother, who, always being in her hut working at her cards, had missed the tale of Great Aunt Thirza's hospital appointment.

Mary, to her great annoyance, blushed. 'Yes—he said that she was able to resume normal life again and that she was very fit for her age.'

'Was he nice?'

'He seemed very nice,' said Mary cautiously.

Polly asked, 'What did he look like?'

Mary longed to describe him in every small detail but that would never have done. 'Oh, well, quite young—he was Dutch . . .'

'But what did he look like?' persisted Polly.

'Very tall and big with gingery hair, only it was grey too, and he had very blue eyes.' She remembered something and smiled. 'Great Aunt Thirza called him "young man"!'

Her father said, 'Your aunt was always outspoken.'

'Did he mind?' asked her mother.

'No, he said that he rather liked it.'

'He doesn't sound like a specialist. Do you suppose that if I'm ill he'd look after me?' Polly looked hopeful.

'Well, no—he looks after people with bad hearts.'

'Supposing you broke your heart—would he look after you?'

Mary said in a level voice, 'No, I don't suppose that he's got time to waste on broken hearts, only ill ones.' She got up from the table. 'I'll bring the coffee in here, shall I?'

*   *   *

Life settled down into its accustomed pattern once more. Mary's days were full. Her father had dropped a pile of notes all over his study floor and it took hours of work to get them in order again; her mother floated in and out of the house, absorbed in her painting, and Polly was away most of the day.

Mrs Blackett, free to do as she liked again, was her usual ill-tempered self, although she no longer threatened to leave, and Mary slipped back into her customary routine. And if her thoughts dwelt wistfully upon Professor van Rakesma she didn't allow them to show; she had plenty of common sense and she was aware that day-dreams, though pleasant, had nothing at all to do with real life.

There was Arthur too. He had been away on a course and now he was back and, though she was reluctant to do so, she had agreed to go out to dinner with him—to a nice little place in Hampstead, he had told her; they would be able to get a good meal very reasonably.

The idea that she was only worth a reasonably priced dinner rankled with Mary, but she got out a pretty if somewhat out-of-date dress, put polish on her nails, did her face and piled her glorious hair on top of her head. She made sure that the casserole for the family supper was safely in the oven, and went to remind her father that she was going out.

He looked up from his writing. 'Out? Well, enjoy yourself, my dear. Have you a key?'

She went down to the hut next. 'I'm going out to dinner with Arthur, Mother. The supper's in the oven; it'll be ready at half-past seven. I've told Polly.'

'Dear child,' said her mother fondly, 'go and enjoy yourself—who with?'

'Arthur.'

'Oh, Arthur, of course. Tell me, do you like robins on this card, or do you suppose a bunch of holly would be better?'

'Robins,' said Mary.

Polly was in the hall. 'I'll see to supper, Mary. Did you feed Bingo?'

The family cat had made himself scarce while Great Aunt Thirza had been there, only skimming in for his meals, but now he was in possession of the house once more, commandeering laps and eating heartily.

'Yes—here's Arthur...'

Polly caught her arm. 'Don't say yes, Mary,' she whispered urgently. 'He might propose!'

'Arthur has never done anything hastily in his life; he'll have to give a proposal a lot of thought, and he'll lead up to it so gradually that I'll have plenty of time to think about it.'

'You like him?'

Mary said guardedly, 'I've known him for a long time, love; he's a good man but I don't want to marry him.' She added thoughtfully, 'I don't think he really wants to marry me...'

Arthur had got out of the car and thumped the doorknocker; she kissed Polly and went to meet him.

Arthur's 'Hello, old girl,' had nothing lover-like about it. She said, 'Hello, Arthur,' and got into the car beside him and enquired about his course.

Telling her about it took up the entire drive and he still hadn't finished when they sat down at a table in the restaurant. It was a pleasant place but not, she decided, the right background for romance. Its pale green walls were too cool, and the white tablecloths and little pot of dried flowers echoed the coolness, but since Arthur obviously had no thought of romance that didn't matter.

Mary ate her plaice, French fries and macédoine of vegetables, chose trifle for pudding and listened to him. She was a kind girl, and it was obvious that he needed to tell someone everything which had occurred at the course. She said 'Oh, splendid,' and 'Really?' at suitable intervals, and wondered what Professor van Rakesma was doing...

She thanked Arthur when he took her back home, offered him coffee, which he refused, and accepted his kiss on her cheek. 'A splendid evening, Mary—we've had a good talk.' He added, in a rather condescending tone which grated on her ear, 'When I can find the time we must do it again.'

What about my time? thought Mary, and murmured politely.

Getting into bed, she decided that in ten years' time Arthur would definitely be pompous.

She was getting the breakfast ready the next morning when the phone rang. Mrs Cox, usually so calm, sounded agitated. 'Miss Mary? The doctor's here; your aunt's took bad. She wants you—ever so restless she is. The doctor said if you could come to ease her mind. Won't go to the hospital, she says, at least not until you come.'

'I'll be there as soon as I can, Mrs Cox. Tell Great Aunt Thirza, will you?'

Mary switched off the gas under the frying-pan and went to find her mother.

CHAPTER TWO

THERE were cars parked on either side of the road where Mrs Winton lived. Mary wedged the elderly Austin into the space between a new Rover and a Rolls Royce and nipped smartly across the pavement and up the steps to the front door.

'I thought you'd never get here,' said Mrs Cox, no longer the silent and austere housekeeper now that she was thoroughly put out. 'Your aunt's real poorly; the doctor's with her now.'

'If she's so ill she must go back to hospital or have a nurse here—where's this doctor?'

'Ah—the niece,' said a voice gently beside her. There he was—the man she had been thinking of all day and every day, standing a foot from her, smiling. 'Mrs Winton's doctor is with her; I thought it best if I were to have a word with you...' He glanced at Mrs Cox. 'If we might go somewhere quiet?'

They were ushered into the drawing-room and Mary sat down on the self-same horsehair chair that she had so happily vacated so short a time ago. She was glad to sit down; she had never believed that nonsense about knees turning to jelly when one was confronted by the loved one, but hers were jelly now.

'Fancy seeing you again,' she said, and added, 'That's a silly thing to say.' And she blushed because he was smiling again, although he said nothing.

He stood by the door, watching her, and presently said, 'Your aunt has had a mild heart attack. Not serious enough for her to return to hospital but she will need to stay quietly at home for a few days. As you may know, the treatment is now quite an active one, but she is old which largely precludes it. If it is difficult for you to stay with her I'm sure Dr Symes will be able to find a nurse from one of the agencies, but I understand from Mrs Winton that you are a very capable young woman, and, of course, a nurse—a private nurse—is a costly expense in these days.'

I don't cost a penny, reflected Mary bleakly.

'There will be very little for you to do,' said the Professor smoothly, watching her expressive face from under heavy lids. 'See that she takes gentle exercise each day, eats sensibly, doesn't become agitated...' Mary gave him a cold look. 'Yes, I quite understand that Mrs Winton is used to having her own way, but she appears to like you and will probably do what you ask of her.'

He came and sat down opposite her on another horsehair chair. 'You are needed at home?' He sounded casually sympathetic. 'You live close by?'

'No, no, I don't; at least, Hampstead isn't far, but it's an awkward journey. Besides, there's no one to see to the house.'

He raised his eyebrows. 'You live alone? I gathered from the hospital that Mrs Winton was staying with a nephew—your father?'

'Yes, but Father's writing a book and my mother paints. My sister's only thirteen and she's at school all day. Mrs Blackett could manage for a day or two, but she's always on the point of leaving.'

'Mrs Blackett?' prompted the professor gently, greatly enjoying himself.

'Our daily. At least, she comes four mornings a week, but—she didn't get on well with Great Aunt Thirza.'

'Just so.' The professor might have been only thirty-five years old, but his manner was that of a man twice his age, seemingly prepared to listen sympathetically and give suitable advice. Mary responded to that; she had plenty of friends of her own age, but it wouldn't have entered her head to bore them with her worries, but here was a sympathetic ear, and it seemed the most natural thing in the world to unburden herself.

'Mother——' she began. 'Mother's a darling, and so clever with a paintbrush, but of course she's artistic and she doesn't really like cooking and that kind of thing; besides, the money she gets for the cards is most useful. And Father's very clever; he doesn't notice what's going on around him. I wouldn't change them for the world but they simply can't manage unless someone is there to see to the house. Polly's splendid, but she's at school and there's homework. So you see it is a bit awkward if I have to stay here...' She added snappily, 'Not that I'm indispensable...'

'No, no,' soothed Professor van Rakesma. 'Of course not, but I see that you have problems. Would it help if you were to go home for a few hours each day? Perhaps while your aunt rests in the afternoons?'

'Have you any idea what the traffic is like between here and Hampstead—the other end of Hampstead?'

He tucked this useful piece of information away at the back of his mind and said that he had a very good idea. 'If a nurse were to relieve you for a few hours each day would that help?' And at her look of surprise he added, 'I'm sure the National Health Service would be prepared to pay for her; she would cost a lot less than having your aunt in hospital, besides giving us another empty bed. Always in short supply.'

'Would they? Who should I ask?'

'Leave that to me. Now, I think we might join Dr Symes and his patient.'

Great Aunt Thirza was sitting, propped up by pillows, in a vast mahogany bed; she looked pale and tired and Mary forgot how tiresome the whole thing was and bent to kiss her cheek. 'I'm sorry, Aunt Thirza, but a few days' rest and you'll be as right as rain.'

'So that foreign man tells me. Dr Symes is of no use at all—nice enough, but of course all doctors are fools, and don't contradict me, miss!' She caught Mary's hand. 'You'll stay, Mary?'

'Until you are better, yes, Aunt Thirza.'

Mrs Winton closed her eyes. 'Then go away and leave me in peace.'

Mary looked at the two men. Dr Symes nodded to her to go with him, leaving the professor at the bedside. Outside the door he said, 'She'll listen to him. Are you sure you can manage? I'll be in every day and I dare say Professor van Rakesma will visit again. It was a piece of luck that I happened to be on the other phone to him when the housekeeper rang up—said he'd seen her at St Justin's and asked if he might come and see her. Very civil of him.'

She agreed, and added sedately, 'I'm sure it will be a great relief to Aunt Thirza to know that she is being looked after so well. You'll be here in the morning?'

'After surgery, but phone me if you are worried.'

They were joined by the professor then, who, beyond wishing her good morning, had nothing further to say before the two men went out to their cars and drove away. She shut the door and went to find Mrs Cox.

'You're staying, Miss Mary? I told the doctor and I'm telling you that I'm the housekeeper, not the nurse. I've

enough to do without fetching and carrying all day and
half the night.'

'Yes, of course I'll stay, Mrs Cox. Professor van
Rakesma thinks that Mrs Winton will be fully recovered
in a short time. I'm sure that it must have been a nasty
shock to you when she became ill again. I'll look after
my aunt so please don't worry; I'm sure that you have
enough to do.'

Mrs Cox bridled. 'Well, as to that, I'm sure I'm willing
to give a hand when necessary—though I won't be left
alone with Mrs Winton.'

'No, no. No one would ask you to do that. I'm sure
we'll manage very well between us. I'll go and see my
aunt now. I dare say she's tired after being examined.'

Great Aunt Thirza was asleep. Mary stealthily opened
a window, and sat down on a little spoon-back chair and
went over her conversation with the professor. He had
said that she was to leave things to him, that he would
arrange for someone to come each day so that she could
go home, but he was a busy man and, however well
meant, she doubted if anything would come of that.

It had been a delightful surprise seeing him again, she
reflected, not that he had been over-friendly. Well, she
conceded, he's been kind and helpful, but she rather
thought that he would be that to anyone with a problem.
She had to admit that he had shown no special interest
in her, but then why should he? Probably he was happily
married...

'Why are you sitting there?' demanded Great Aunt
Thirza. 'There's surely something you can be doing? I
don't approve of idle hands.'

'I was waiting for you to wake up,' said Mary. 'Dr
Symes wants you to have a warm drink—tea or milk
or cocoa?'

Great Aunt Thirza was feeling cantankerous. 'I don't want a drink...'

Mary got to her feet. 'I'll bring you a tray of tea—Earl Grey—and do you fancy a little fish for your lunch?'

'Fish! Fish? I'm very ill, girl, probably dying...'

'Professor van Rakesma said that you will be up and about in a few days. You've had a nasty fright, Aunt Thirza, but there's no question of your dying. A nice little piece of sole, with a morsel of creamed potato and perhaps a purée of new peas?'

'You may bring it to me,' said the old lady ungraciously, 'but I shall most likely be unable to eat it.'

It seemed a very long day to Mary; her aunt kept her busy, for she was a bad patient, prone to do exactly the opposite to what she was asked to do, so that Mary got into bed quite worn out with hanging on to her patience. She had phoned her mother that evening, and was relieved that everything was going smoothly at home—although Mrs Pagett's efforts at cooking supper seemed to have been rather chaotic.

'You won't have to stay there long?' her mother had asked.

'No, I don't think so.' She recounted what the doctor had said but didn't mention the professor's offer to find a relief for her each day. It had been a kind thought, she reflected sleepily, but he would have forgotten by now.

He hadn't though. Mary was carrying her aunt's lunch tray downstairs the next day when Mrs Cox admitted an elderly woman in a nurse's uniform.

Mary, poised on the bottom tread of the stairs, stared at her. 'He actually meant it,' she exclaimed.

The woman smiled. 'Indeed he did. Professor van Rakesma seldom says much, but when he does he means it. He has arranged for me to come each day while you are here—two o'clock until half-past five.'

Mary put down her tray and shook hands. 'That's very kind and thoughtful of him—and kind of you too. It's not interfering with your work? I didn't realise that the Health Service were so helpful.'

'Well, you must have time to yourself. I'm Maisie Stone.' She glanced at Mrs Cox, who was standing by the door looking rather sour.

'This is Mrs Cox, my aunt's housekeeper,' said Mary hastily. 'She runs the house beautifully and is such a help.'

Mrs Cox looked smug. 'I'm sure I do my best but, as I told Miss Mary here, I won't do no nursing or lifting or suchlike.'

'Well, I wouldn't expect you to do that,' said Mrs Stone comfortably. 'I'm sure we shall get on very well together.' She turned to Mary. 'If I might take a look at the patient?'

Ten minutes later Mary was in the car, driving home. It was an awkward journey, but she had discovered several short cuts and the traffic wasn't too heavy and it was worth it; her mother was delighted to see her—it wasn't one of Mrs Blackett's days and the kitchen needed urgent attention. Mary put on a pinny. 'If you'll make us a cup of tea—there's a cake in the tin on the dresser—I'll just clear these dishes and saucepans. What had you planned for the evening?'

'There's that chicken you were going to roast...'

'I'll casserole it. Then all you'll have to do is put it in the oven a couple of hours before you want it.' Mary picked up a teatowel. 'Mother, supposing I write down what you need to buy each day? Then when I come home I'll get it ready to cook.'

'Oh, darling, would you? I've been so busy I've hardly had a moment to do any painting. Perhaps Polly...?'

'Well, no, love, she's got a lot of prep to do when she gets home, hasn't she? If you pop down to the shops each morning you'll have the rest of the day to work—you and Father can have a cold lunch. Is he at home?'

'No. He said he'd be back about five o'clock.'

Mary hung the teacloth to dry and sat down at the table. 'So we'll have tea and decide what to buy tomorrow.'

'Will you be away long?' asked her mother wistfully. 'We don't seem able to get on very well when you're not here, dear.'

'Not long, and I can come home each afternoon—well, most of them; I don't know about weekends.'

But when Sunday came Mrs Stone arrived at her usual hour, and this time the professor was with her. He took a quick look at Mrs Winton, pronounced her greatly improved, suggested that she could take some exercise each day and, as they went downstairs, observed casually that since he had heard that Mary lived at Hampstead, and he was on his way there, he would give her a lift.

Mary paused on the bottom tread. 'Thank you; that's kind of you to offer but I've got our car—I have to get back again, you see.'

'I'm invited to tea with my godson—his parents live near the Heath. I'll pick you up at around five o'clock and collect Maisie.'

Even though she was so much in love with him and could hardly bear him out of her sight Mary took a few moments to agree to this. Her heart might be his, but common sense told her that allowing herself to get involved wouldn't do at all. A prudent refusal was on the tip of her tongue when he said, 'Well, run along and get your coat and we can be off.'

He sounded just like the older of her two brothers; besides, if she refused to go she might never see him again...

She went out to the car with him and he opened the door for her to get in. There was a dog sitting behind the steering-wheel—a Jack Russell, white and black with a whiskered face full of intelligence. He eyed her beadily and the professor said, 'A friend, Richard,' and went round to his door and got in.

Richard moved to sit between them, panting and uttering short happy barks. Mary rubbed his ears and asked, 'Why Richard? It's an unusual name for a dog.'

'He has a lion's heart. Don't let him crowd you; you like dogs?'

'Yes, but we haven't got one. We have a cat called Bingo.'

He began to talk about her aunt then; he sounded exactly like a family doctor, which made him remote so that she couldn't find the courage to ask him about his work, let alone his personal life. Even though he talked about Mrs Winton it was surprising the amount of information he gleaned from her without giving the least inkling of his own life.

They were very nearly at her home when she asked shyly, 'Do you live here in England or go back to Holland?'

'My home is in Holland but I spend a good deal of time here.' He added lightly, 'A foot in either camp, as it were.'

Which left her knowing no more about him than that.

He stopped before her home and she thanked him with a hand on the door ready to jump out, but he was there before her, holding her door open—something Arthur wouldn't have dreamt of doing even if she'd had her arms full of parcels. Arthur would have sat behind the wheel and said, 'So long, old girl.'

Professor van Rakesma was older and wiser than Arthur, besides the fact that he had nice manners. He opened the gate, glanced at the shabby house with its elaborate gables and said, 'There must be a splendid view from the back of your home.'

'Oh, there is—the Heath, you know.'

They stood facing each other, either side of the gate, and he smiled suddenly. 'I'll be back around five o'clock, Miss Pagett.'

She went up the overgrown drive to the front door and turned round to look when she reached it. He was still there, and she wondered uneasily if he had expected to be asked in. He had said that he was going to have tea with his godson... She opened the door and went inside.

Polly came into the hall to meet her. 'Mary, I haven't seen you for days. Mother's in the hut and Father's in the study. I cooked most of the lunch. Can you stay for tea? I made some rock cakes.'

'Lovely, Polly, and I can stay for tea, but I have to be ready to leave at five o'clock.' She went on with a slightly heightened colour, 'I have a lift here and back.'

'Not Arthur?'

'Heavens, no. What I mean is, I don't think he knows I'm at Aunt Thirza's house.'

'Then who?'

'Professor van Rakesma brought Mrs Stone, who relieves me each day, and since he was visiting someone in Hampstead he said he'd bring me home and drive me back.'

'What's he like? I know you said he had ginger hair and blue eyes but is he nice?'

'Very nice.'

'Is he married?'

'I really don't know. He's—he's not a man to talk about himself, I think.'

'Well, then, he's a nice change from Arthur,' observed Polly. 'It would be nice if he fell in love with you and married you, and that would be one in the eye for Arthur.'

'Arthur is a good, steady man,' said Mary as they went into the kitchen and began to gather things ready for tea.

'Oh, pooh,' said Polly. 'Can you imagine what he'll be like in ten years' time?'

Mary knew exactly what she meant.

On Sundays, when they were all at home, they had tea in the drawing-room—a large, lofty-ceilinged place and very draughty since the old-fashioned windows were ill-fitting and allowed the air to seep in round their frames. In winter, of course, the door was shut and no one went near the place; it would have cost a fortune to light a fire large enough to warm the room and there was a damp patch in one corner which dried out during the summer and reappeared each autumn.

Today was dry and warm, however, and the room, though shabby and on the chilly side, was pleasant enough; the chairs were elderly but comfortable and Mary and Mrs Blackett kept the tables and cabinets polished. They laid the tea things on a table by the big bay window at the back of the room and Mary cut sandwiches while Polly cut the cake and boiled the kettle.

As Mary sliced and spread she allowed her thoughts to wander. Professor van Rakesma was probably at that very moment eating his tea somewhere in Hampstead. It would be a more elegant meal than she was preparing, of course—good china and silver teaspoons and cake-stands. He must be glad to get away from the hospital, which was jammed tight among narrow, busy city streets. Would he live there? she wondered, and dismissed the idea. Consultants would only be at the hospital at certain times; he must have a flat...

'Mary.' Polly had raised her voice. 'I've been talking to you for ages and you haven't heard a word. Are you in love? You look quite moony.'

'Good heavens, no.'

Mary spoke so sharply that Polly said, 'Well, you don't have to snap my head off. P'haps you are tired. Great Aunt Thirza's pretty grim, isn't she?'

'She's old. Will you be a darling and fetch Mother from the hut? And I'll get Father.'

Tea was a pleasant, leisurely meal. Mrs Pagett wondered in her dreamy way when Mary would be home again, and her father remarked in a vexed voice that when she was away he could never find anything that he wanted.

'I'll be home soon,' soothed Mary. 'Aunt Thirza is much better and she's to start doing more tomorrow.'

'That's nice, dear. Don't let her tire you too much,' observed her mother. 'I suppose you have to go back after tea?'

'Yes. Five o'clock. Professor van Rakesma gave me a lift here and is calling for me then.'

'He could have come to tea...'

'He was going to have tea with his godson, some-where in Hampstead.'

'Will he be coming in? I still have one or two cards——'

'He won't come in, Mother. I'll wait for him at the gate—he'll want to get back.'

Mrs Pagett got up. 'Then you won't mind if I go back to the hut and get on with my painting, darling. I'll see you tomorrow, I expect.'

She wandered away down the garden and presently Mr Pagett got up too. 'I'll leave you two to tidy up; I'll only be in the way.'

Polly ate the last sandwich. 'I'll wash up,' she volunteered, 'after you've gone.'

'We'll do it together—there's fifteen minutes before he'll be here.'

They cleared the table together and went into the kitchen. Mary turned on the sink taps and waited patiently for the water to get warm—the boiler was beginning to get temperamental—and Polly went off to feed Bingo. She went out of the back door to call him in and found him lying comfortably in a rose bed by the gate. Professor van Rakesma was leaning over the gate, doing nothing.

'Hello,' Polly danced up to him. 'Have you come for Mary? She's in the kitchen, washing up.' She scooped up Bingo and added, 'Open the gate and follow me.'

The professor smiled down at her. 'Shall I be welcome?'

'Why ever not? If you're a professor shouldn't you be old or at least elderly?'

'Er—you know, I'd never thought about it. I shall, of course, in due time be elderly and hopefully old.'

'How old are you?'

'Thirty-five.' He sounded amused.

'I'm thirteen. Mary's twenty-four, getting on a bit; if she doesn't marry Arthur she'll be an old maid.'

'Then let us hope that there is an alternative.'

They had arrived without haste at the kitchen door and he stood for a moment watching Mary, who was attacking a saucepan with a great deal of energy so that her hair was coming loose as she rubbed and scoured. She didn't see him at once but when Bingo let out an impatient miauw said, 'You found him. Good. I can't think why this saucepan is burnt—what...?'

Something made her turn her head then. Feeling very much at a disadvantage, and aware that she hardly looked her best, she said peevishly, 'You should have come to the front door.'

He said meekly, his heavy lids hiding the gleam of amusement in his eyes, 'I do apologise. I'll go back and ring the bell while you tuck your hair up and assume your usual calm manner!'

She smiled then, and Polly laughed. 'I'm sorry—I didn't mean to be rude.'

'Think nothing of it; I am convinced that a burnt saucepan is enough to upset any housewife worth her salt.'

Polly said suddenly, 'I like you. You're not a bit like a professor. Are you married? Because if you aren't you might——'

Mary, with a heightened colour, interrupted her briskly. 'Polly, be an angel and tell Father I'm just going, will you?' She was washing her hands and wishing that she could get to a comb and a looking-glass. Heaven alone knew what she looked like. 'I'll get my handbag...'

Polly went with them to the car and the professor waited patiently while she admired it. 'I've never ridden in a Rolls Royce,' she observed wistfully.

'Then I will come and take you for a ride one day.'

'You will? You promise?'

'I promise.'

'You're great—I do wish that Mary——' She caught
her sister's look of outrage and went on airily, 'Well,
perhaps I'd better not say that.' When they were in the
car she poked her head through the open window. 'If
you take a good look at Mary she's quite pretty!'

The professor spoke gravely. 'I agree with you absolutely, Polly.' He waved goodbye and drove off and Mary,
very red in the face, was relieved when he didn't even
glance at her.

She said presently, 'You mustn't take any notice of
Polly—she's a bit outspoken.'

'One forgets how delightful it was when one could
speak honestly—something quickly smothered by the
conventions. Have you ever considered how much
happier we would be if we uttered our real feelings instead of the well-mannered platitudes expected of us?'

'Well, it would be nice sometimes to say just what one
wished to say...' She stared ahead of her. 'I expect you
have to—to—wrap up your words to your patients.'

'Indeed I do, but if I'm asked a straight question then
I give an honest answer.'

'You like being a doctor?'

He smiled faintly. 'Yes, it has been, until very re-
cently, the one great interest in my life.'

She thought about this. 'Are you going to get
married?'

'Shall we say, rather, that I have from time to time
considered it?' He glanced at her. 'And you?'

'Me? No...' She cast around to find some light-hearted
remark about that, and was relieved when Richard,
perched between them, decided that her lap would be
more comfortable. After that they said very little until
he stopped at Great Aunt Thirza's front door.

After he and Maisie had gone Mary, preparing her aunt's supper since Mrs Cox had gone to church, allowed her thoughts to dwell on the professor. His goodbye had been polite but uninterested, just as though, she thought bitterly, he had discharged a task and was thankful that it was done. Well, she would take care to keep out of his way in future; she would badger Dr Symes to allow her to go home within the next day or two.

She carried out her plan on the following morning when Dr Symes arrived. There was really no reason for her to stay any longer; Great Aunt Thirza was quite recovered, she told him. Dr Symes agreed.

'I can arrange for a practice nurse to come in each morning, just to keep an eye on things, and both Professor van Rakesma and I are agreed that the sooner your aunt returns to her normal, quiet way of living the better. You do understand that there may be further heart attacks, but living an invalid's life is no guarantee against that?'

'So it would be quite all right for me to go home in a day or two? Of course I'll come over and see my aunt—I could come each day if you thought that I should—but I really need to be at home...'

'Yes, of course; shall we say the day after tomorrow?'

Mary told Maisie that afternoon. 'I expect Dr Symes will tell Professor van Rakesma, won't he?'

Maisie nodded. 'Sure to—after all, the professor was consulted in the first place, although of course your aunt is Dr Symes's patient. Don't worry, my dear. You could stay here for months and your aunt would be as fit as a fiddle, on the other hand she could die tomorrow; you never know with heart cases, and she is an old lady.'

As if in complete agreement with Maisie's words, Great Aunt Thirza died peacefully in her sleep that night.

It was Mary, taking her an early morning cup of tea, who found her. She put the small tray she was carrying slowly down on to the bedside table. The cup rattled in the saucer because her hands were shaking but she stayed calm, aware of regret that the old lady had died and at the same time glad that her end had been so peaceful.

She wasn't going to pretend to a sorrow she didn't feel; Great Aunt Thirza had been a difficult and despotic member of the family, but all the same she had been family. Mary murmured a childish prayer and went to phone Dr Symes.

Mary had plenty to occupy her for the next few days. Her father reluctantly undertook to make all the necessary arrangements, but she and Mrs Cox were left to deal with all the details. Maisie had come, alerted by Dr Symes Mary supposed, and proved invaluable, but although Mary's father had dealt with the undertakers he had left a great deal for her to do.

'I've let Aunt Thirza's solicitor know,' he told her. 'He'll see to everything, my dear. The funeral is on Friday; did I tell you?'

'No, Father. Do you want everyone to come back here afterwards? It's usual. Mrs Cox will see to that side of things.'

'Do what you like, Mary. I told the solicitor to let any friends know.' He smiled briefly. 'I don't think your Great Aunt Thirza had many.' He added vaguely, 'She was twelve years older than my mother and the last of her generation.'

He patted her arm, 'Well, my dear, I think I've seen to everything. Arrange things with your mother, won't you? I have an appointment later on today...'

There weren't many people at the funeral other than the family. There was Mrs Cox, of course, tight-lipped and dour in black; she had said little to Mary but Mary guessed that she was worried about her future—she had been with Great Aunt Thirza for many years and another job might be hard to find now that she was past middle age. There were several old ladies there too—Great Aunt Thirza's bridge companions. They said little, but ate Mrs Cox's splendid tea with relish.

It was when they had all gone that Mr Shuttleworth, Great Aunt Thirza's solicitor, observed that he would now read the will. He was an old man, and Mary, who had a vivid imagination, thought that he looked as if someone had taken him out of a cupboard and dusted him down for the occasion.

Great Aunt Thirza having been Great Aunt Thirza, her will held no pleasant surprises. Mrs Cox was to have the contents of the wardrobe and two thousand pounds, Mr Pagett three thousand pounds, Polly the full set of *Encyclopaedia Brittanica* and Mary an early edition of Mrs Beeton's cookery book, with the hope that by its perusal she might improve her cooking.

The house, its contents and the remainder of her not inconsiderable fortune were to be given to various charities.

Mrs Pagett received nothing, which caused her no distress at all. Great Aunt Thirza had never approved of her designing Christmas and greetings cards; she had once observed that it was no suitable occupation for a lady. Mrs Pagett, even if she was whimsical, didn't lack spirit; she had laughed and muttered, 'Pooh,' before going away to her shed.

Mary watched Mr Shuttleworth tidy away his papers. It was a pity that Great Aunt Thirza hadn't left her father a larger portion of her fortune. All the same, perhaps now the roof might get a few necessary tiles and the old boiler could be replaced with something modern. She saw Mr Shuttleworth to the door, her mind busy with domestic problems.

CHAPTER THREE

IT WAS days later, when Mary took the household bills to her father, that he told her that he didn't intend to pay them. 'That is to say, of course, they will be paid, but they can easily be left for a few weeks. My credit is good...'

'I do need some petty cash, Father—Polly's bus fares and Mrs Blackett—and the window cleaner is due this week.'

He frowned. 'Yes, yes, of course, Mary. Your mother had a cheque this morning; ask her to let you have whatever you need—I'll repay her.'

Her mother, absorbed in the painting of Christmas elves in a snow scene, told her to find her handbag. 'It's somewhere in the bedroom, Mary—there's some money there. Take what you need, dear, and let me know how much so that I can get it back from your father.' She paused for a moment and looked up. 'Are we short of money?'

'No, Mother. I need some petty cash and Father hasn't enough.'

She didn't like running up bills at the local shops but, as her father had pointed out, they were known to the local tradespeople and his credit was good. All the same, at the end of another week, when the butcher asked for something on account Mary waylaid her father as he prepared to leave the house.

'I'm already late,' he told her testily. 'I have an important appointment—very important.' His testiness was

45

suddenly replaced by a broad smile. 'Be sure that I'll give you the money you require this evening, Mary.'

With that she had to be content. There was no need to worry, she told herself. It would be some weeks before her father received Great Aunt Thirza's bequest, but when he did she could settle up the bills.

She frowned, for even without that money there had always been enough—just enough—for her to run the household. It hadn't been easy, but with careful management she had contrived, but now, mysteriously, her father's private income seemed to have dwindled; she had been told to borrow from her mother's purse once more, and she knew for a fact that until the next batch of cards was sent away there would be very little money left in it.

She went along to the kitchen and found Mrs Blackett scowling.

'Met yer pa in the hall,' she said angrily. 'Told me I don't need to come no more—give me the sack, 'e 'as.'

'The sack? Mrs Blackett you must be mistaken...'

'Course I'm not; I got ears, ain't I? What I wants ter know is, why?'

'I've got no idea. Could you forget about it? For I'm sure he didn't mean a word of it. I'll see him when he gets home this evening and I'm sure everything's all right.'

She glanced at Mrs Blackett's cross face. 'Let's have a cup of tea before you start on the kitchen. I'll get the washing machine going and make the beds.'

Mrs Blackett, mollified, drank her tea—strong with a great deal of sugar—and began on the kitchen, and Mary loaded the washing machine and went upstairs. There was something wrong, something amiss somewhere, and she wished she had someone in whom she could confide.

There wasn't anyone—Polly was too young, Arthur would be bored and impatient, her mother wasn't to be worried, she decided lovingly, and the only person she really wanted to pour out her doubts and troubles to was miles away, gone for good.

Indeed, Professor van Rakesma was miles away, in Holland. He hadn't, however, gone for good.

Her father usually came home around five o'clock when he'd spent the day at the British Museum, had a cup of tea and went straight to his study to work on his notes until supper. So Mary was surprised when he arrived home in the middle of the afternoon. She went into the hall to meet him with the offer of coffee or a late lunch, but the words died on her lips. Mr Pagett, never a robust man, had shrunk inside his clothes; a man in his fifties, he had aged twenty years.

'Father—you're ill.' She took his coat and hat. 'Go and sit down in the study; I'll bring you a cup of tea— better still, if there's any whisky left you'd better have that first. I'll ring Dr Hooper.'

'No, I'm not ill, Mary, but I'll have that whisky. I have had some bad news.'

She went with him to the study, fetched the whisky and sat down near his chair. 'Do you want to tell me, Father? Or shall I fetch Mother?'

'No, not your mother, not until I can think of what is to be done. She mustn't be upset...'

He told her then, about a man he had met at the British Museum, researching for a book he was writing about ceramics. 'He seemed a very pleasant fellow, who knew several of the people I had known at Cambridge—or so he said, and I didn't think to doubt him. Mentioned my book on the Dead Languages, asked about the book I'm writing now; in fact we became friendly.

'Some weeks ago he told me that he had a brother in the Stock Exchange who occasionally gave him tips. There were some shares coming on the market, he said, at a rock-bottom price; if I had some capital lying idle it would be a very sound investment. It seemed a splendid way in which to use Aunt Thirza's little windfall. I said that I had three thousand pounds to invest and gave him a cheque—yes, I know I haven't received my bequest yet but I withdrew some of my capital; this investment he was to make for me was going to earn twice as much interest.

'He showed me the listed shares in the *Financial Times* and indeed the price was going steadily up. He suggested that I might like to put another thousand or two to the first investment and I withdrew another six thousand.'

Mary said slowly, 'So that's nine thousand pounds...'

Her father said heavily, 'He has gone—this man— together with the money. The shares he showed me had nothing to do with it; he probably guessed that my knowledge of them is negligible.'

'So you have to repay the bank with Aunt Thirza's money?'

'Indeed, yes, and over and above that I shall have to employ a solicitor to take the matter to court.'

'What is the use of that if the man has gone, Father? Probably he's in Australia or South America by now. Did you report it to the police?'

'Yes, yes, of course, and they tell me that there is almost no chance of reclaiming the money.'

'We'll manage,' said Mary in a voice she strove to make cheerful. 'After all we always have, and you've still got the income from your investments.' She gave him a re-assuring hug. 'Besides, your book will be finished in another six months or so, won't it?'

'My dear, you do not know the whole. Some of my shares have fallen; we have been living from capital for some months now. I have not yet had the time to go into the matter thoroughly, but my income is sadly depleted. We must cut down on expenses. I'm sure that you can do that; you manage so well.'

Mr Pagett was looking better; whisky and the comfortable knowledge that Mary would cope as she had been doing for years had somewhat restored his peace of mind. He would leave everything to her. He patted her hand and said vaguely, 'We'll say nothing—eh, my dear? And now I have some notes to write up, and I'm sure you have the supper to cook.'

It was too early to start the supper; her mother was still painting and Polly was in the dining-room, doing her homework. Mary sat down at the table and allowed herself the luxury of feeling scared and doubtful.

No way could she be more economical than she was now. They could sell the car, she supposed, but that would mean fares each time anyone had to go somewhere. They could give up Mrs Blackett, but she quailed at the prospect of running the place unaided; it was a large and awkward house, and she lacked the modern appliances to make running it easier.

'I'll get a job,' said Mary aloud. 'Mrs Blackett can stay, and I can get up earlier and go to bed later.' She frowned, 'What kind of job? It'll have to be close by, and part-time if I can earn enough. Mother's help? A shop? Housework?'

Mother's help, she decided, and, having done so, instantly felt better. After all, it need only be for six months or so; once her father's book was published everything would be all right.

Feeling quite cheerful, she went to the fridge—the remains of the lamb joint they had had could be turned into a shepherds pie. The sight of it reminded her that the butcher wanted to be paid—she would have to get a job as soon as possible.

She scanned the local paper the next morning and saw with satisfaction that there were several advertisements for mother's helps, all of them local. She cut them out and decided to phone them all for an appointment.

She put the phone down after her fourth call—full-time, she had been told, and no dependents. The next call was more promising—part-time, ten in the morning until four o'clock in the afternoon, Sundays free, sixty pounds a week and her midday dinner. Two children, said the voice. Four years old and five, boy and girl, lively and happy. The voice made an appointment for that afternoon and rang off.

Sixty pounds a week, reflected Mary, and it was only a short bus ride—one of the large houses overlooking the Heath. She could pay off the tradespeople, keep Mrs Blackett, and lay out the rest of the money as economically as possible. The reluctant thought that she hadn't much liked the voice she decided to ignore.

Her father was out, her mother absorbedly painting and Polly not yet back from school. Mary, very neat, and hoping that she looked like a mother's help, got on to a bus.

The house was just as she had expected—large, red-brick and solid, with a big garden separating it from the road. She rang the bell.

The door was opened by a small, thin girl in a grubby apron and suffering from a heavy cold. 'Come on in,' she invited, not waiting for Mary to speak. 'The missus is expecting you.'

The girl opened a door in the large hall. 'In here—Mrs Bennett, here's the young lady.'

She padded off down the hall and Mary walked into the room. It was as she had secretly feared—the person matched the voice. She was a handsome young woman, if one didn't mind the small eyes and the down-turned mouth, dressed in the height of fashion and wearing too much jewellery.

She was sitting in a deep chair by the window and said pleasantly enough, 'Come in and sit down. I do hope you'll do; the children are utterly charming, but they're rather out of hand and I'm not much good with them. Have you brought your references with you?'

'No, Mrs Bennett, but I can give you the names and addresses of several people who will vouch for me.'

'You live in Hampstead?'

'On the other side of the Heath.'

'So you can get here by ten o'clock each morning? I go out a good deal—you'll see to the children's dinners, of course. No housework—there's a daily woman as well as Maggie, who opened the door to you. She lives in. I expect you to keep the children amused and clean and tidy—and a walk every day; I'm a great believer in fresh air.'

'They don't go to school?'

'No, Ben's five, but he's highly strung, and Grace is only four. Come up to the nursery and meet them.'

The nursery was up two flights of stairs, behind a baize door, and the two children were throwing toys around the room as they went in.

'They are so high-spirited,' said Mrs Bennett, and dodged the stuffed rabbit that her small son flung at her. 'They get bored and Maggie can't control them.'

Mary eyed them; the boy was big for his age, dark and too plump. He would grow into a handsome man, she decided, but perhaps not a very nice one. She resisted the impulse to stick her own tongue out in response to his and looked at Grace. A small girl, with light brown hair and large blue eyes, she was snivelling and her nose needed wiping. Mary felt a rush of pity for her; she needed a bath and clean clothes and her hair needed washing.

Maggie did her best, no doubt, but Mary suspected that she had more than enough to do in the house. She followed Mrs Bennett downstairs again, and was told that, provided her references were satisfactory, she could start in two days' time—a Monday.

'You'll be paid weekly,' said Mrs Bennett. 'It's an easy job and well paid.'

Mary murmured politely; she didn't think it would be easy and she wasn't sure that it was well paid, for she knew no one with a similar position, but it was the straw that the proverbial drowning man clutched at. Perhaps it wasn't quite what she had hoped for but the thought of being able to look the butcher in the eye and pay him at the end of the week sent her spirits soaring.

She caught the bus home, her eyes sparkling, her pretty face alight with relief, so that the other passengers took a second look at her—to see someone so obviously pleased with life on a London bus was unusual and heart-warming.

Some of her euphoria ebbed away when she reached home. She had already decided to tell her mother that she felt the urge to do more than be at home all day; a little outside interest would be nice, she would say, and her mother would agree placidly. Her father would tell her to do whatever she wanted, his clever head so full of his learned book that he would have quite forgotten that if she hadn't done something about it they would have been in a sorry way.

Not that she blamed either one of them; they were made that way, content with each other and their lives, never allowing unpleasantness to interfere with the placid way of life. The boys were no longer at home, Polly was nicely settled at her school, and Mary saw to everything...

It was Polly who would ask questions and raise objections, and Mrs Blackett, once more installed as the household help, would certainly have her say. Mary rehearsed suitable answers for the pair of them and hoped for the best.

'It's not fair,' blazed Polly when she was told. 'You ought to be out every night, dining and dancing in pretty dresses with someone super like Professor van Rakesma; I bet he'd take you somewhere grand and you'd eat caviare...'

'It's only for a few months, Polly—Father was deceived into putting money into bogus shares; it really wasn't his fault and I don't mind a bit. I always have time to spare during the day; it'll be fun to be paid for using it up.'

'You're fibbing. I think it's beastly for you—you can have my pocket money...'

'Thank you, love; that's very generous of you, but I'll have some pocket money each week, truly I shall.' She began to improvise, to rid her sister's face of its look of doubt. 'If Arthur asks me out I'll be able to go and have my hair done...'

'Arthur,' said Polly with scorn. 'I wouldn't waste my money on a decent hair-do for him!'

Mrs Blackett, when told the following morning, was outspoken. 'It's not for the likes of me to ask why you should go gallivanting round the place with a parcel of children, as though you 'aven't enough to do 'ere. I'll not deny I'm glad ter be coming as usual, but extra time I can't and won't offer; I've got that old Mrs Caldwell two afternoons a week and Mr Trevor on Fridays—it's as much as I can manage.'

'If you'd just come as usual, Mrs Blackett, I'm sure we can cope. It's only part-time.'

'There's part-time and part-time,' said Mrs Blackett, 'and a very elastic thing it can be, as you'll no doubt discover, Miss Mary.'

Mrs Blackett was always gloomy, reflected Mary. It wasn't going to be as bad as she had hinted; in fact, it would be a splendid way of solving the temporary problems which had arisen so swiftly and unexpectedly.

Only later, in bed in the shabby room she had slept in for years, did she allow her thoughts to return to the professor. It was silly to spend time thinking about him but it was difficult not to, since he was indelibly printed on to her brain. She wondered if in time she would be able to forget him, if he would become dim in her memory. Of one thing she was quite certain: Arthur— indeed any man—would never take his place.

Arthur came the next day. Mary had just got back from church and was wrapping an apron around what Polly called her 'Sunday dress', preparatory to cooking the midday dinner, when he parked his car by the front door and walked in.

'Thought we'd go for a drive,' he said, strolling into the kitchen. 'I need to relax; I've had a busy week. Cut some sandwiches, Mary, and we'll be off.'

He hadn't said, 'Hello, Mary,' or asked how she was, or even if she wished to go with him. She didn't, and she bade him a cool good morning.

'I'm cooking the dinner, Arthur; I can't drop everything and come just like that.'

'Polly can cook, for heaven's sake.' He added bossily, 'Come on, old girl.'

'I may be a girl but I'm not yet old,' she said tartly. 'Besides, I don't want to; I haven't the time...'

He laughed. 'Rubbish. You're here all day with nothing much to do.'

She let that pass. 'There are things I have to do today,' she told him evenly. 'I'm starting a job tomorrow.'

'A job? Whatever for?'

'You have just reminded me that I am here all day with nothing much to do—I think a job will be rather interesting.'

Arthur frowned. 'Well, when we're married don't think you're going to be a career woman.'

'Is this a proposal?' asked Mary, and prodded the potatoes, turned down the gas and turned to face him.

He looked awkward. 'Well, no, I'm not ready to marry yet. It's something which needs careful consideration; I need another year or two before I settle down.'

'I might possibly change my mind within the next year or two,' said Mary gently. She emptied a bowl of peas into a pan of boiling water. 'In fact, Arthur, I think I've changed it now, so you won't need to worry about whether you're ready to marry me or not.'

'I say, old girl, you don't mean that? I'd got quite used to the idea of our marrying when it was convenient.'

'I do mean it. You see, Arthur, when I marry it won't be because it's convenient but because I'm so in love that I can't imagine being anything else but married, if you see what I mean.'

'Good Lord, what's come over you, Mary? You're not behaving normally.'

'Yes, I am. Arthur, dear, go away and find another girl—someone young enough not to mind waiting until you're ready to marry her.' She left the stove and went and kissed his cheek. 'Go along to the rectory; Millie's home for the weekend and she's had her eye on you for months.'

Arthur looked pleased. 'Yes! Well, I might just call in. Mind you, I'm deeply hurt, Mary.'

'Yes, Arthur—all the more reason to have a soothing companion to help you get over it. Millie's very soothing.'

He had been gone for ten minutes before Polly came into the kitchen. 'I've been up in the attic looking for a bit of old blanket for Bingo's basket; Aunt Thirza threw the other one away—she said it smelt. I heard a car...'

'Arthur. He wanted me to go out with him...'

'Well, why didn't you? I know he's not a bit exciting—anyone less sexy...' declared Polly. 'You could have had a super meal somewhere.'

'He wanted me to cut sandwiches.'

'Sandwiches? Is that man mean? Don't marry him, Mary, will you?'

'No, love. He didn't exactly propose, but he wanted to put me on hold until he felt like marrying me, so I refused him and told him to go and find someone else.'

Polly stared at her. 'You don't mind?'

'Not one little bit. Nor, I think, did he. Will you get Mother and Father? Everything is ready.'

* * *

Going home again on the bus after her first day at Mrs Bennett's, Mary wondered for a brief moment if she had been wise to reject Arthur's ideas for their future.

She had set out that morning all agog to make a success of her job. She hadn't known what to expect, although she had been cheerfully optimistic—she would get to know the children, enjoy taking care of them, playing with them and reading them stories, and seeing that they ate their meals.

It hadn't been like that at all. The untidy little maid had let her in and told her that she was to go straight to the nursery. 'She's not up yet,' she had observed, and sniffed. 'Took her breakfast up not half an hour ago. The kids 'ad theirs in the nursery.'

The nursery had been a shambles; the children had been left to eat alone, that was obvious; moreover Grace had had an unfortunate accident and wet her knickers, and Ben was spooning the remains of his cornflakes over the floor.

Mary had done the obvious—cleaned Grace, led Ben away to wash his face and hands and then set about restoring order to the room. The house had been so quiet that they might have been alone in it, the three of them. Presumably Mrs Bennett had still been in her room, and the little maid had had enough to do without Mary bothering her for information. She'd found the children's bedroom—the beds unmade, clothes all over the place—sought for sandals, put them on protesting small feet and had led the children downstairs.

'Where are we going?' said Ben and kicked her ankle.

'For a walk.' If ever a child needed his bottom smacked, Ben did. Perhaps if she walked for long enough and far enough they would both tire and be easier to manage.

The Heath was just across the road; she kept to the more frequented paths and presently let them run free and, sure enough, as they tired they became more manageable, so that by the time they reached the road again they were behaving like normal small children.

Mary, waiting to cross between the traffic, was hot and tired and longing for a cup of coffee. Her hair was coming loose from its French pleat and she was sure her nose shone. Professor van Rakesma, driving past, blinked and looked again. What on earth was the girl doing, clutching two children and looking a good deal less serene than usual? It was a pity he had no time to stop and find out. Mary didn't see him, which, seeing that she felt herself not to be looking her best, was a good thing.

Mrs Bennett was up when they got back. 'I expect to be told when you take the children out,' she observed coldly.

'If you had been here to tell I would have done so,' said Mary reasonably. 'The children were in the nursery; they had eaten their breakfast alone, Ben was throwing the cornflakes about and Grace had needed the lavatory and there had been no one to help her... It seemed the best thing to do was to clean them up and take them out on the Heath.'

Mrs Bennett had the grace to look uncomfortable. 'I overslept. They had better have their morning milk. I suppose you want a cup of coffee...? They have their dinner at half-past twelve and then they're supposed to rest for an hour. I suppose you can find something to do—have you made their beds and tidied the room?' She caught Mary's eye. 'Well, no, I suppose you haven't had the time—you could do that later. I'm going out to lunch and do some shopping. I'll be back before four o'clock.'

The rest of the day went quickly enough—too quickly in fact; it seemed that she was to be responsible for the children's clothes and their bedroom, as well as the nursery where they ate their dinner. She helped Maggie carry it upstairs, and although she was hungry there was little opportunity to eat since Ben, unlike his small sister, was determined to do everything he could to be obnoxious.

Mary, who hadn't taken to Mrs Bennett, nevertheless was relieved to see her a few minutes after four o'clock.

At home she set about preparing the supper while Polly, just back from school, made the tea. 'What was it like?' she wanted to know.

'Quite interesting...' Mary was at the sink, peeling the potatoes.

'Were they awful, the children? Did you have them all day?'

'Well, yes. They did rest for an hour after their dinner—I read to them.'

'It's not as nice as you hoped,' observed Polly. She poured the tea. 'Here, drink this, Mary—tell me about it; Mother and Father needn't know.'

'Well, it wasn't too bad. In fact, if I can tame the little boy and get organised I might quite like it.' She smiled suddenly. 'I shall like it on Saturday when I get paid.'

It would be all right once she had got used to the job, she told herself as she got into bed and lay thinking about the professor until she went to sleep.

He was the first thing she thought of when she woke too, but there was no time to moon around. She got up

and crept downstairs and started on the necessary
housework.

It was a lovely morning—the birds were singing, the
Heath beyond the garden looked delightful and the early
morning traffic was just a distant hum. She made a mug
of tea and took it on to the back doorstep. The professor
would still be in bed, she reflected; probably he had spent
the previous evening at some grand house as a dinner
guest or had dined with some charming girl.

Mary gulped down her tea and went back to dusting
the sitting-room—an occupation which allowed for free
thought. Of course he lived in a splendid flat somewhere—and perhaps had a girlfriend. Her imagination
took off...

The professor was shaving, making a good job of it with
the cut-throat razor held in a steady hand. Despite the
fact that he had been up most of the night, called to the
bedside of an eminent public figure who had suffered a
severe heart attack, he was preparing for another busy
day at the hospital.

He was tired—there were lines of weariness etched in
his handsome face—but presently he went down to
breakfast, to all outward appearances a man who had
had a good night's sleep and the leisure to don the su-
perbly cut grey suit and fine silk tie. He looked pleasant
and impersonal—a man to be trusted.

He had little time for breakfast, but while he ate it he
wondered about Mary. But only briefly—he had a long
day ahead of him and there would be no time to indulge
in private thoughts. Beyond deciding to find out more
about her when he had the time to do so, he dismissed
her from his mind.

*   *   *

Tuesday was only slightly better than Monday. True, the children had been given their breakfast in the kitchen with Maggie but she had too much to do to bother with them. Mary took them to the nursery, dealt with their needs, sat them down at the table with picture books and crayons and nipped around tidying the place, making their beds and collecting their clothes for the washing machine. By then Mrs Bennett had come into the nursery.

'You can take them for a walk now, Mary—while they're resting after lunch you can do the ironing. I've guests for lunch; you'll see the children are up here, won't you?'

She kissed the children and went away again, ignoring Grace's whimper of 'Mummy'. Ben hadn't looked up from his crayoning. Mary's charming bosom heaved with indignation; they were by no means little cherubs, but Mrs Bennett was their mother—surely she loved them.

She had no doubt that they would be quite delightful children if they weren't so neglected. It wasn't wilful neglect. They had nice clothes, their food was exactly what it should be, they had more toys than they could play with—but they hadn't got their mother's love, not all of it anyway. They needed cuddling, laps to sit on, a mother to romp with sometimes. Ben was five years old, but despite his aggressive ways she guessed that he was a lonely child.

As if to bear out her thoughts he was more aggressive than ever that morning... All the same, she walked them across the road and on to the Heath, this time with a ball in her pocket. They soon tired of tossing it about and suddenly Ben took to his heels and ran towards the thicket some way off. 'Stay where you are,' said Mary to Grace, and went after him.

She ran well and he was no match for her long legs. She caught him easily enough and marched him back, not saying anything even when he delivered a few kicks on her shins and tried to bite her hand.

Still without a word she took them home, tidied them up for their dinner and sat them down to eat it.

'The lady who looked after us before you came smacked us,' volunteered Grace, shovelling mince into her small mouth.

'She called Mummy "an old cow",' observed Ben, giving Mary a sidelong look, puzzled because she hadn't seemed to mind his running away.

'That was rude and I don't want to hear you say it again, Ben. You're not a baby; you must behave like a boy—you'll be going to school soon with other boys.'

'I don't care...'

'Don't care was made to care, don't care was hung, don't care was put in the pot and cooked till he was done,' said Mary, which sent the children off into peals of delighted laughter.

'Aren't you cross?' asked Ben as she settled them on their beds.

'Not in the least. Close your eyes and go to sleep, my dear.' She tucked the quilt round Grace's small face and left the door open while she did the ironing in the nursery.

Tea was a peaceful meal and she had left soon afterwards, anxious to get to the shops before she went home. She was tired but the day had been no worse than the previous one, and tomorrow was Wednesday, halfway through the week, and on Saturday she would be paid.

The week wound to its close with its few ups and far too many downs, but she forgot that in the satisfaction of paying the butcher's bill. There was very little money left in the housekeeping purse; she added her wages to it, assured her father that she would manage very well without asking him for her usual allowance—even though she knew that he had no intention of offering it—paid Mrs Blackett, gave Polly her pocket money and sat down to plan the housekeeping for the next week. Provided that no bills came in, she could manage.

Halfway through the next week Mrs Bennett put her head round the nursery door as Mary was clearing up after the children's breakfast. No one, it seemed, thought it necessary to collect the plates and mugs, wipe the children's faces and hands and tidy the room. At first she had resented it but, since Maggie had more than enough to do and Mrs Bennett didn't rise from her bed until ten o'clock, she had accepted it as something that would have to be done whatever she felt about it.

To see Mrs Bennett up and, moreover, dressed in the height of fashion was a surprise; she was quite taken aback when that lady said briskly, 'Get the children decently dressed, Mary; I've an appointment for them with my dentist. You will come with them, of course. You can have twenty minutes while I get the car and see Maggie.'

It needed patience and strength to coax the children into clean clothes. Grace, being small and female, had no objection to wearing one of her prettier frocks and her red sandals, but forcing Ben into a shirt and shorts and his favourite trainers without actually causing him bodily harm was quite another matter.

All the same, by the time Mrs Bennett called sharply for them to go down to the hall Mary had achieved her purpose. There would be a few bruises on her shins and a few nasty scratches on her arms later on, but that was neither here nor there.

Mrs Bennett drove a Mercedes, and, ordered on to the back seat with the children, Mary wondered once again if her employer had a husband. Was she divorced, or did he work away from home? she wondered. It wasn't her business, of course, but it would be nice to know...

Mrs Bennett drove well and rather too fast, and she didn't speak at all until, some time later, she stopped outside one of the tall red-brick houses in Harley Street, put money into a parking meter and told Mary to get out and bring the children with her.

Naturally the pair of them hung back—Grace in tears because she didn't understand why she was there and Ben kicking and screaming since that was his normal behaviour when faced with a situation he didn't fancy.

Mary had reached the dignified entrance when the door was opened to Mrs Bennett's ring and she swept inside to the elegant vestibule. There were two men standing to one side of it and Mrs Bennett paused and smiled charmingly at them, secure in the knowledge that she was a handsome woman beautifully dressed— although the effect was rather spoiled by her son bawling his head off.

She said over her shoulder, far too sharply, 'For heaven's sake, Mary, control the children. Really, you must manage them better than this.'

She made a pretty little grimace, shrugged and looked at the two men again. The elder of them wasn't worth more than a glance but his companion... She tried to catch his eye but he was looking past her, his face without expression.

Mary, wrestling Ben into the vestibule, had been too occupied to look around her. Mrs Bennett's waspish remark had filled her with rage and her cheeks were flushed; her wish to turn round and go out into the street and leave her employer and her children to fight it out between them was so overpowering that she had to clench her teeth together and remind herself that at the end of the week there would be another sixty pounds.

She took a firmer grip of Ben's hand, soothed the weeping Grace, and looked up to encounter Professor van Rakesma's cool stare.

CHAPTER FOUR

MARY'S instant delight at the sight of Professor van Rakesma gave way to embarrassment; she was already hot-cheeked; now the slowly ebbing colour crept back, giving him the chance to admire it. She blushed charmingly, and that, combined with eyes blazing with her rage, turned her into an arresting beauty.

What good fortune had sent her here for him to meet again so unexpectedly? he wondered, and gave her a smiling nod. It was the smiling nod he gave to his patients, courteous and impersonal, and Mary, recognising it as just that, gave him a stiff, unsmiling nod in answer as she went past him.

Of course he had gone when, after a trying hour, she got into the car with Ben and Grace, both weeping and scarlet in their faces with childish rage.

Mrs Bennett was disposed to be friendly. 'That's over for another year,' she observed over her shoulder. 'Why the children have to make such a fuss I don't know. They'll be home late for their dinners, but that can't be helped. They've had enough excitement for one day; they can go straight to rest once they've eaten. They don't need to go out again. Give them their tea before you go, Mary.'

It didn't enter her head to say please or thank you. 'Did you notice that man in the vestibule as we went in? Not the old one, the other one—I wonder who he is? I might be able to find out; I wouldn't mind meeting him sometime.' She added defiantly, 'One gets lonely when one's husband is away for weeks at a time.'

It was a remark that Mary decided it was better not to answer.

Thankfully the children were too tired to be naughty; even Ben settled down to take a nap after his dinner, leaving her free to tidy up and finish the ironing, which was an occupation conducive to thought, she had discovered. It had been exciting and delightful to see the professor again, and in such an unlikely place. Perhaps he had been to the dentist too? With a spurt of tenderness she hoped that he hadn't had the toothache.

Professor van Rakesma had watched Mary disappear into the dentist's waiting-room, bade his companion a civil goodbye and had taken himself up to the floor above, where he had his consulting-rooms.

It was only when the last of his patients had left that he allowed his thoughts to dwell on her.

It was obvious to him that she must give up her job and find something more congenial. He had no doubt that beneath her patient handling of the little boy she was hiding a desire to smack his bottom. Professor van Rakesma, who liked children, had considered Ben to be a holy terror much in need of parental discipline.

He wondered idly if there was a Mr Bennett and just how long Mary would stay there. There must be a good reason for her having to do so...

His receptionist put her head round the door to tell him that she was off home. 'You're booked solid tomorrow,' she warned him cheerfully, 'and the first patient is that nervous Mrs Payne.'

'Ah, yes . . .' He bade her goodnight and began to consider the nervous Mrs Payne, and he thought no more
about Mary.

Mary received her sixty pounds at the end of the second
week, feeling that she had earned every penny of it and
more. She had made progress with little Grace, although
she cried a great deal and showed no interest in her toys—
expensive dolls with wardrobes, a doll's house of mag-
nificent proportions, and any number of picture books.

But what use were they, reflected Mary, when there
was no mother around to play with her and a bullying
brother who took pleasure in breaking her things? But
once or twice Grace had smiled, even laughed, and they
had had a splendid time spring-cleaning the doll's house
together, despite Ben's efforts to interfere.

Ben, she considered, needed to go to a strict pre-prep
school where there would be other children to cut him
down to size. He was a tyrant now; what he would be
like as he grew older she shuddered to think. All the
same, she had to stay; the sixty pounds was a lifeline
until things got better at home.

She said nothing to her mother and father about her
job, giving them the impression that it was all rather
fun; only Polly guessed that it was far from ideal. Mary,
starting her third week, allowed herself the luxury of
day-dreaming on the bus. She had done her best to forget
Professor van Rakesma but somehow he wouldn't go
away; besides, she found it comforting to think
about him.

He hadn't given her another thought. His days were full
and so were his leisure hours; besides, he was starting
on a learned book about cardiac arrest—something

which was dear to his heart and taxed his very clever brain—so that everything which had nothing to do with that received scant attention.

Meeting Polly on the following Saturday morning on the Heath reminded him of Mary once more.

Polly was with friends, but she spied him at once, striding along with Richard racing ahead, and she ran to meet him.

'I knew I'd see you again one day,' she told him happily, 'and it's all right about not having come to take me for a drive; Mary said you might not have enough time and I dare say you haven't.'

He stood looking down at her cheerful young face wreathed in smiles. 'Mary is quite right; I have been very busy.' He glanced around him. 'You're alone?'

'No, with friends. I'm not allowed to come here by myself, but they're over there; I can catch them up easily.'

She threw a twig for Richard. 'Mary's got a job, looking after two horrid children on the other side of the Heath. The little boy is simply beastly; he bites her and kicks her and yesterday he cut her with a knife he'd found. Not a bad cut, but it bled on to her only decent skirt. I suppose you couldn't do anything about it?'

'I? I'm sorry your sister has such an unpleasant job but I can hardly interfere. Surely she is capable of changing jobs and getting something more to her liking?'

'Of course she is. But jobs aren't that easy to get and she has to get some money...' She paused. 'I'm not supposed to talk about it,' she mumbled.

He gave her a kind smile. 'You know, people tell me all kinds of things when they come to see me; it relieves their minds, you see, and I forget everything they have said. I think if you want to talk to me about it it will be quite in order. I'll forget it too.'

She stared up at him, nodded and said, 'I think that, inside you, you are a very nice man. It would be nice to tell you, and Mary won't know...

'You see, Father was cheated of almost all his money; Great Aunt Thirza left him some too, and the man took that as well. It wasn't really Father's fault; he's very clever and writing a book and he forgets about things. Mother's clever too, but she doesn't worry about money. So Mary got a job so that we could go on living...'

She added fiercely, 'But I know she hates it although she never says so.' She put a hand on his sleeve. 'You won't tell anyone, will you?'

He said gently, 'No, Polly, you have my word. I'm not going to promise that I'll help her, because I can't see how I can, but if I should hear of anything more suitable I will let you know.'

'How?'

'A letter would be best, but don't be too hopeful. I haven't forgotten our drive either; maybe I'll just turn up and hope that you are at home.'

'Oh, great! You really are rather nice. I don't suppose... No, of course not.' She had gone rather red. 'I'd better go before the others get too far away.' She put out her hand. 'Thank you very much.'

They shook hands and she ran off, and he stood and watched her rejoin her friends in the distance before he resumed his own walk. For a little while he thought about Mary, regretful that there was little that he could do.

In that he was mistaken; two days later, browsing in the bookshop he frequented—a dark, low-ceilinged series of rooms housing literary treasures—he came upon its owner, an elderly man, untidy as to dress, wearing old-fashioned spectacles on his long, thin nose and with a wreath of white hair surrounding a bald patch.

They wished each other good day and the old man said, 'There are some more interesting books I've just received—part of a private library. Unfortunately I haven't had the time to unpack them. My assistant has left suddenly in order to be with his mother, who lives, I believe, somewhere in the south of France. I have advertised in various journals but so far I have had not one applicant. I am not sure how I shall manage.'

Professor van Rakesma said slowly, 'Indeed, how unfortunate. Must your assistant have qualifications of any kind?'

'Qualifications? No, no. A willingness to please the customers and learn something of my trade. Well-spoken, of course, and honest.'

Professor van Rakesma observed, 'I believe that I may be able to help you. A young lady, educated—you may know her father by name—Pagett . . .'

'Indeed I do; erudite and a great scholar. If she has a fraction of his learning I would be more than pleased to give her employment.'

'I'll see what I can do,' said the professor, and wondered what he was letting himself in for. Ten to one, if Mary discovered that he was instrumental in finding her a job she would refuse, not wishing to be beholden to anyone, certainly not him.

All the same, later that day, sitting in his drawing-room with Richard's whiskery chin on his shoes, he pondered his chances. It was past midnight when he went to bed, tolerably satisfied with his plans.

Polly, mooning around the garden on the following Saturday afternoon, was enchanted to see Professor van Rakesma making his way up the short drive to the house. She ran to meet him. 'I knew you'd come.' She paused.

'But perhaps you want to see Mary? She's working this afternoon because Mrs Bennett wanted to go out; she won't be back until after tea.'

'I came to see you, Polly. Shall we drive around for a while; there's something I want to discuss with you.'

'A secret?'

'Yes, but a nice one, I think. Do you need to tell someone where you will be?'

'I'll tell Mother but she'll forget—shall we be gone long?'

'No, I want to be gone again before Mary comes home.'

'Two ticks,' said Polly, and raced along to the hut to tell her mother.

Only when she was sitting beside him in the car did she ask. 'Why don't you want to see Mary, Professor van Rakesma?'

He was driving north towards Mill Hill. 'I'll explain...' Which he did, in a few clear, business-like sentences. 'And this is what I would like you to do—I have a cutting of old Mr Bell's advertisement in my pocket. Would you let Mary see it? Say that you saw it and wondered if it would be more fun than the Bennett children. On no account must you mention me...'

'Why not? Are you in love with Mary?'

He answered coolly, 'Not in the least, Polly. But I have seen her twice with those children, and it was obvious on both occasions that they were making her life a misery.'

Polly nodded. 'She won't talk about it; you see, we haven't any money unless she has a job, and Mrs Bennett is starting to make her work longer hours.' She added, 'It's a pity you're not in love with her because then you could have married her and she wouldn't have had to work again.'

He gave her a smiling, sidelong glance. 'Two people have to love each other if they wish to marry—at least, that is the ideal theory. I admire your sister for the way she is tackling your troubles but there is no love lost between us, Polly.'

'Oh, well...that's a pity. You'd have done very nicely; it's not easy for her to find someone that's taller than she is. She's on the big side...'

'Indeed,' he agreed, 'she is!'

They had reached Mill Hill, and he drove on for a short distance until they reached a roadside café where he stopped. 'An ice, perhaps, before we go back?'

Polly polished off the ice, and since he had thoughtfully ordered a plate of cream cakes with the tea-tray she ate most of those as well.

Back in the car, she said, 'I like your car, and thank you for taking me for a drive and for that lovely tea. Mary makes fairy cakes at the weekend, but they're not the same, are they?'

'They sound delightful. Tell me about your school, Polly. What do you want to do when you are grown up?'

'I'd like to be a vet, but I don't suppose there will be enough money for me to train; I mean, even if I got trained for free there's still clothes and things... I could be a veterinary nurse, though; that's the next best thing.'

They discussed the future at some length until they were back at her home again, and Polly was delighted when Professor van Rakesma got out of the car and held the gate open for her.

'It was lovely,' she told him and leaned up. 'Bend down so I can kiss you.' She patted her pocket, where the advertisement lay hidden. 'I'll do just as you say and I won't breathe a word. Shall I let you know if she gets the job?'

'I know the gentleman who owns the bookshop; I expect he will tell me, but you can let me know if you wish. Send a letter to the hospital—St Justin's.'

He waited until she had gone indoors and then drove away.

Ten minutes later Mary got home. She had stayed for two hours over her usual time because Mrs Bennett had wanted to visit friends for lunch and spend the afternoon with them. She had come back late, without apologising, paid Mary her sixty pounds and had asked her if she would come an hour earlier on Monday morning.

'I must get my hair done, and that means going into town and you know what the traffic's like at that hour of the morning, so be here punctually, will you?'

'It is difficult for me to come any earlier than ten o'clock,' Mary had said.

'Good gracious, girl, surely you can oblige me this once? This is an easy job and I pay you well. I'll expect you.'

Mrs Bennett had gone to her room. Mary had fetched the overworked Maggie to sit with the children and had taken herself off home, her temper in shreds.

Which, of course, was ideal from Polly's point of view, although she said nothing about the job at the bookseller's until they had had supper and the pair of them were washing up in the kitchen.

'Was Mrs Bennett beastly?' she asked.

'Yes, rather. And I have to go in earlier on Monday because she's having her hair done. I think she must have guessed that I need the money and don't dare leave...'

Polly flung down her towel. 'That reminds me, Mary, I was looking at the magazines and journals in the library when I went to change my books and I saw this in one of them. No one was looking so I cut it out...'

'Where did you get the scissors?'

'I had my sewing-bag with me—you know I do sewing on Saturday mornings.' She fished in her pocket. 'Here, read that.'

Mary dried her hands and, leaning against the sink, studied the short advertisement. 'It sounds nice— Thursday, Friday and Saturday—I wonder how much I'd earn. It's all day away...'

'Well, you're almost all day away now, aren't you? And you'd have four days at home. Oh, Mary, do write— at least find out about it.' She added, 'You like books too...'

'Perhaps I will,' said her sister slowly. 'I wonder whereabouts it is.'

'Write and find out,' said Polly.

So Mary wrote her letter and posted it without much hope of getting a reply, which made it all the more exciting when she had one asking her to call for an interview at her convenience. The bookshop was open all day except for Sundays, and the owner was always there.

'It's miles away, though—in one of those funny little streets behind Oxford Street. I suppose I could get the underground to Oxford Circus.'

'It's only Tuesday,' said Polly, gobbling her breakfast. 'Go straight there from Mrs Bennett's; he won't shut before five o'clock—you'd have heaps of time.'

'Well, yes, I suppose I could.'

'Of course you could. I'll be home before then; I can start the supper if you're not back. Do go, Mary; it might be the chance of a lifetime.'

So Mary went, rather tired—after hours with Grace and Ben—but with her nose nicely powdered, her pretty mouth lipsticked, her hair smoothed into its chignon and her shoes well polished with one of Mrs Bennett's shoe-brushes.

The shop was where she had thought it would be, hidden away in a narrow street, away from the bustle of the shops in Oxford Street. It was an old house, one of a row of old houses, their small shop windows filled with antiques, old pictures and fine silver. There was a stamp collector's paradise too, next door to the bookshop. She opened the door and an old-fashioned bell tinkled some-where at the back.

There were several people inside and she stood for a moment, wondering which one was the proprietor, until an elderly man touched her arm. 'You will be Miss Pagett?'

'Yes, yes, I am. You are Mr Bell? You don't mind me coming like this without phoning first?'

'Not at all. Come this way, young lady.'

He led her to a tiny cubby-hole at the back of the second room. 'Sit down, my dear, and tell me why you want to work for me.' He added, 'I know of your father—a brilliant man of letters.'

'Yes, he is, isn't he? He's almost finished his book.'

'Which will bring him fame if not fortune! Now, if you will tell me something of yourself—your education and present employer, if you are employed.'

He listened without interrupting. When she had fin-ished he observed, 'I think that you may suit me very well. Shall we agree on a month's trial? Three full days; that is from nine o'clock in the morning until five o'clock each evening, and on Saturdays until six o'clock. Half an hour for lunch—I have an arrangement with a nearby café who will send in coffee and sandwiches. You will not pay for these, of course. Mid-morning coffee and mid-afternoon tea when we can fit it in. I will pay you eighty-five pounds a week if you are agreeable to that?'

Mary did some rapid and not very accurate mental arithmetic. Even with fares she would be better off. 'Thank you; that suits me very well. I do have to give a week's notice... If I do that tomorrow morning I should be able to start here on Thursday week. Will that do?'

'Admirably.'

They parted, well-pleased with each other, and Mary, oblivious to the crowded underground, did hopeful sums in her head. She would have two lots of wages next week, she reflected happily. She smiled at the thought, and the sour-faced woman strap-hanging within inches of her gave her an outraged look. There was no call for smiles going home in a packed underground train after a long day.

Mr Bell waited until he had shut his shop for the day before telephoning Professor van Rakesma. 'A very pleasant young lady,' he observed in his dry old voice. 'She will suit me very well; I am most indebted to you for recommending her.'

'I'm glad you are satisfied. I would regard it as a favour if you would not tell her that it was I who recommended her.' He didn't enlarge on this, and Mr Bell didn't ask for an explanation.

Home again, Mary went straight to the kitchen, where Polly was doing her homework at the table and keeping an eye on the macaroni cheese in the oven. She looked up as Mary went in. 'Well—have you got the job?'

'Yes, starting next week—on Thursday. Oh, Polly, it's twenty-five pounds more and a free lunch. I'd better tell

Father and Mother, and I'll have to fix things so that you can all manage the supper if I'm not home...'

'Oh, don't fuss, Mary; if you leave everything ready I'll manage. I can cook.'

'Yes, love, I know, but you have your homework. I'll prepare things and put them in the freezer. After all, I've four days at home to do it.' She hugged Polly. 'Oh, love, it's such a relief.'

'You'll have to give notice.'

'Tomorrow morning. I must write a letter and give it to Mrs Bennett.'

'She'll be mad...'

'I think so too, but she'll have a week to find someone else, and anyway she could look after Ben and Grace herself.'

She went to look at the macaroni cheese. 'Supper's almost ready. Shall I keep it warm while you finish your homework?'

'Let's have it now; I'll fetch Mother from the hut if you will tell Father.'

Over supper Mary told them that she had a better job. 'Someone who knows of you, Father. A Mr Bell; he has an antiquarian bookshop behind Oxford Street.'

'Old Bell! Well, I never did! He has some splendid books; you'll enjoy working there, my dear.'

'A nice quiet job for you, darling,' said her mother. 'And how convenient that will be; you can take the cards up to my agent. Think of the time I shall save, and I hate the journey up to Bloomsbury.'

Mary agreed cheerfully, and wondered when she would find the time to go there—something she could worry about later, she decided. And presently she sat down to compose a letter of resignation.

Mrs Bennett read it the next morning, a look of unbelieving rage on her face. 'Why, you ungrateful girl. After all I've done for you, leaving at a moment's notice—where am I to get another girl in a week, I'd like to know?'

'An agency?' suggested Mary helpfully. 'There must be any number of girls wanting a job.'

'Don't be ridiculous, Mary. Anyone from an agency would want more money...' She shot Mary a quick glance. 'That is, I doubt if there's anyone around here, and they would want money for fares. Anyway, I consider it very deceitful of you.'

'Deceitful? I've given you a week's notice, Mrs Bennett, as soon as I was offered this other job.'

Mrs Bennett sneered. 'A likely tale. Well, work your week out, and don't come here wanting your job back when you don't find this new one to your liking.' She stared at Mary, her good looks marred by ill temper. 'That's the worst of you half-educated girls—can't settle down in a decent job when you've got it. No wonder you haven't got a husband,' she added spitefully.

Mary, with a great effort, held her tongue.

Leaving the house for the last time a week later, Mary heaved a great sigh of relief. Mrs Bennett had made life as unpleasant as possible—going out of the house the moment Mary got there each morning and on her return finding fault with anything and everything. The children were dirty, she said, and too noisy; they hadn't had their proper meals, they had been made to walk too far... Her complaints had been endless. Mary, with a tremendous effort, had still held her tongue.

She had no time to get nervous about her new job since it was to start the next morning. She did some important shopping on the way home and, while the supper cooked, prepared meals for the following day and then went in search of her mother.

She found that lady with her paints. 'There you are, dear—I don't seem to see much of you these days. Do you suppose cherubs and Christmas roses would go nicely together? Red, white and green, I thought—pink cherubs, of course...'

Mary peered over her shoulder. 'They are sweet, Mother; they'll be a huge success. Look, dear, I shall be away all day tomorrow, Friday and Saturday. The new job, you know. I'll put all the food in the freezer and you'll find everything for lunch in the fridge. Polly will be home around five o'clock, and I should be back by six o'clock.'

'Your father says Mr Bell is a scholar of the first order; you'll enjoy yourself, Mary, I'm sure. We'll manage, your father and I.' She smiled up at her daughter. 'We are so used to having you to see to everything—we've been selfish, I think. When I've finished this batch of cards I'll look around for a husband for you—invite some young people to the house. We might even have a party...!'

Mary gave her a hug. 'Sounds fun, but there's time enough to get me married. I'm sure when your agent sees these he'll come up with another order.'

The shop door had a 'Closed' sign on it when she got there the next morning but as she tried the door it opened and she went in. Mr Bell's reedy old voice, bidding her good morning, came from the back of the second room, and she walked through to find him in his little office, unpacking a box of books.

'Sit down, Miss Pagett, and catalogue these as I unpack them. It is too early for customers, and I cannot put them on the shelves until they have been entered.'

He pushed a massive book towards her. 'I have started...'

So she sat down without preamble and did as he bade her, and all the while he talked between reading out the authors and titles. 'Some first editions,' he told her happily. 'Not well-known authors, but I have regular customers who collect early nineteenth-century writers.'

They worked together for half an hour or more, and when a customer came into the shop he left her to finish entering the last few books. After that he took her round the shelves so that she had some idea of how the books were classified. 'Don't worry if you are unable to help a customer; just fetch me, Miss Pagett.'

She nodded her head. 'Mr Bell, would you call me Mary? No one ever calls me Miss Pagett—well, the butcher does!'

'I shall be glad to do so, Mary—such a pretty, old-fashioned name. Now, go and make the coffee for us both. There's a small pantry through the door there.'

By the end of the day she knew that she was going to like her work. The shop was dusty and rather dark but it had atmosphere, and the people who came to it were unhurried, with time to browse, and would sometimes go away again without buying anything.

She had taken the money and wrapped books for three customers without mishap, putting the money in a drawer behind the small counter. It would have been the easiest thing in the world, she reflected, to lean over and take the money and run, but she reassured herself with the thought that the customers who came to the shop didn't look the type to rob the till.

The next day was going equally well and then, as she minded the shop while Mr Bell had his lunch, Professor van Rakesma walked in.

She was on her knees, rearranging a shelf of books so near to the ground that no one seemed to have noticed them for a long time, judging by the thick layer of dust on them, but when the doorbell tinkled she looked up.

The professor stood in the doorway, his vast person blocking what light there was. He stood without moving for a few moments, watching her as she scrambled to her feet. At length, he said, 'Miss Pagett? Working here?' His surprise was exactly right—careless, amused, not very interested. 'You have difficulty in finding a job to suit you, perhaps?'

Mary stared at him. How was it possible to love a man who was so tiresome? He hadn't even bothered to wish her good day. She said coldly, 'Good afternoon, Professor van Rakesma. Yes, I am working here. Do you wish to see Mr Bell, or have you come to browse?'

'Both. I'll browse until Mr Bell is free. There are some first editions, are there not? Came this week. Any idea what they are?'

She had taken the trouble to look at them all carefully; she might not know much about the authors but she had remembered their names and some of the titles. 'They are early nineteenth-century, from the library of a house in Shropshire.' She recited some of the authors and he raised his brows.

'You've been doing your homework.'

'I work here,' she told him, still cold. 'They are over there—the second shelf on the left. Mr Bell won't be long.'

He nodded and went to the shelves, and she turned her back. The dusty shelf would have to be finished now that she had started on it. Thank heaven there were no customers to show up her ignorance. She glanced at her watch; Mr Bell would soon be finished, leaving her free to take his place in the office and eat her own lunch, and by the time she had finished Professor van Rakesma would be gone.

Mr Bell came presently and saw him at once. 'Ah, one of my most valued customers. Mary, go and have your lunch while I show him my latest find.' He peered round the shop until he saw her on her knees by the obscure shelf. 'There you are. Run along now.'

She felt about twelve years old when he spoke like that. She rose to her not inconsiderable height and went meekly without a word. He was a nice old man, but could he not see that she was a grown woman of Junoesque proportions, unlikely to run along when bidden? She felt a fool, and probably the professor was laughing.

Her half-hour wasn't quite up when Mr Bell poked his head round the door. 'If you could come. I know your half-hour isn't up, but there are several customers.'

No professor, however. He had gone just like that, she thought pettishly; he could have called goodbye, or said something kind about her job, or asked after Polly. I shall stop loving him, she reflected, knowing that that wasn't going to be possible.

She'd had no idea that an antiquarian bookshop could be so busy; she received money, handed over change and parcelled up books for most of the afternoon. She wasn't of much use selling, but at least she allowed Mr Bell the freedom to talk to his customers and show them his treasures. Hopefully in a few weeks she would be of more use to him.

She was managing quite nicely, he had told her, but she knew that if she wanted to keep the job she would have to learn a great deal as quickly as possible. She closed the door on the last customer and went to fetch her jacket.

Mr Bell was pottering about, putting back books taken off the shelves. 'A good day, Mary, and we shall be busy tomorrow—Saturday. A different kind of customer, though. I'll see you in the morning. Goodnight.'

She wished him goodnight too, and he locked the door as she went out. It had been a warm day and the late afternoon was still pleasant, but the streets were crowded with people going home and the traffic was a steady roar.

She took a breath of moderately fresh air and almost choked on it as Professor van Rakesma, appearing apparently from the ground at her feet, said briskly, 'The car's round the corner. I'm going to Hampstead; I'll give you a lift.'

She found her voice. 'Oh, you startled me. That's kind of you, but I can get home easily on the underground.'

'Don't talk nonsense—it's the rush hour. Come along.'

She went with him, telling herself that she was a weak fool and at the same time happy to see him again. For the last time, she reminded herself sternly as he ushered her into the comforting depths of the Rolls's front seat, shut her in and went round the bonnet to get in beside her.

He drove off without fuss and without speaking, and she watched the people hurrying along home and tried to think of something to talk about. Perhaps it would be better to stay silent until they were clear of the worst of the traffic. She was still making up her mind when Professor van Rakesma spoke.

CHAPTER FIVE

'I MUST find the time to take your sister for that drive I promised,' said Professor van Rakesma. 'Will she be at home on Sunday—some time in the morning? Your parents wouldn't object to her coming with me? We might have lunch somewhere.'

Lucky Polly, thought Mary. 'I'm sure they wouldn't mind, and Polly will be over the moon. It's very kind of you; I don't suppose you have a great deal of leisure.'

'Not a great deal, no. How long have you been working for Mr Bell? You left the lady with the two children?'

'This is my second day.' She added defiantly, 'And I like it; I hope I shall be able to stay and get to know a great deal about books. Yes, I left Mrs Bennett; the children were a bit difficult. Perhaps I'm not cut out to look after them.'

'My dear girl, the sternest of matrons would have found those two a handful. Did the dentist subdue them?'

She smiled. 'For the rest of the day, yes. I hope they get a nice, kind mother's help whom they'll like.'

'They sound like orphans...'

'They need someone to love them.'

His gentle grunt was soothing.

When they reached her home he got out to open the door and then the gate to the drive. 'Thank you for the lift. Shall I ask Polly to come out and you can tell her yourself? She'd like that.' She went pink. 'That's awfully rude; I didn't mean it like that. Please come in and see her.'

The problem was solved by Polly, running down the drive. Mary turned thankfully to her. 'Polly, Professor van Rakesma has invited you to go for a drive...' She held out a hand and had it engulfed in his large cool one. 'Thank you again; I'll leave you to arrange things.'

When she had gone into the house Polly said breathlessly, 'Mary doesn't know that I've already been out with you?'

He smiled and shook his head. 'I've given myself a day off on Sunday; I thought we might go a little further afield this time. Do you suppose you could persuade her to come too? I think a day in the country might do her good.'

'Oh, she'd love it.' Her face clouded. 'But I'm not sure that she'd come; she's always there on Sundays, to see to the dinner and get tea for Mother and Father.'

'Well, do your best; perhaps we can persuade her between us.'

Polly swung on the gate. 'Well, will you bring Richard?'

'Most certainly—he likes the country.'

He said goodbye then, and drove away, and Polly went indoors. She was a wise child; she said nothing about Mary's going with them on Sunday.

Professor van Rakesma drove himself back home, wondering what had possessed him to suggest spending a Sunday with a teenager and her stand-offish sister. He could, he reflected, have spent it in the company of friends, or driven himself to the little cottage in Gloucestershire, to potter in its small and beautiful garden with Richard for company. He shrugged his shoulders, turned the car into Cheyne Walk, and stopped before the handsome Regency house where he had a flat.

His man came into the hall as he went in. He was a young man, with a pleasant but ugly face and a thatch of fair hair. 'Evening, sir. Your mother's been on the phone; she said she'd ring around eight o'clock. Dinner in half an hour?'

The professor was leafing through his post. 'Please, Fred. It's your evening off, isn't it?'

'S'right. Me and Syl are going to see that new film at the cinema.'

'Splendid. Has she named the day yet?'

'Boxing Day—got to wait a bit, haven't I? But you'll be in Holland, sir, and by the time you get back we'll be nicely settled in—looking forward to it, she is. Hope there'll be enough to keep her busy...'

'I've no doubt you'll find something.' He looked up, smiling. 'Something smells good.'

'Beef *en croute*—just about ready. I've put the drinks in the sitting-room. Richard's in the garden.'

Professor van Rakesma opened a door at the back of the square hall and entered his sitting-room, a pleasant place comfortably furnished with deep armchairs, small lamp-tables, placed where they were most needed, and glass-fronted cabinets on either side of the Adam fireplace.

He crossed the room and opened the door leading to a small garden beyond, and Richard came bounding in to sit at his feet while he had a drink and finished reading his letters. The last one he read slowly, and then read again.

It was from someone he had known for a number of years in Holland; Ilsa van Hoeven and her husband had been friends of the family, and when they had divorced she had continued to see the van Rakesmas. She was a charming woman, good-looking and most intelligent, and she made no secret of her warm feelings towards him. He supposed that one day he might marry her. It was time that he settled down and she would be a suitable wife.

The thought crossed his mind that he didn't particularly want a suitable wife, but he dismissed it, finished his drink and crossed the hall to the dining-room, to sit at the oval table with its gleaming silver and elegant china and eat his dinner.

Presently, with Fred gone and the house quiet, he went to his study to work on his book until after midnight. In the morning he would go to the hospital to check on several of his patients and if he wasn't called to an urgent case he would drive down to the coast to dine with friends.

Mr Bell had said that it would be busy on Saturday, but all the same Mary was surprised at the constant flow of customers. They ignored the expensive first editions and rare volumes, asking for books on fishing, sport of all kinds, history and old maps, and there were a few young women looking through turn-of-the-century books on costumes and manners of that period.

Somehow she scrambled through the day, and when the last customer went through the door she said apologetically, 'I'm afraid I wasn't much use, Mr Bell.'

'On the contrary, you were a great help to me; besides, you have the right temperament. This is the one shop where customers refuse to be hurried, and I saw that you realised that.' He handed her an envelope. 'You will suit me well, Mary. I hope that you will stay with me, although I suppose a pretty creature like you will marry and leave me!'

'Well, I have no one in mind at present,' she told him, her fingers crossed because that was a whopping lie if ever there was one. 'I like working here very much, and I'll learn all that I can as quickly as possible.'

'Good, good. I'll see you next Thursday.' He bade her goodnight and locked the door behind her, and she made her way home, tired and rather hungry. Not that that mattered. She had eighty-five pounds in her purse, and money meant security for another week. It wasn't only that which made her feel happy; she had seen Professor van Rakesma the day before.

Perhaps it was the afterglow of that happiness which made her agree almost without hesitation to go with Polly when he called for her on Sunday morning. She had no reason to stay at home, for her mother and father were having lunch with friends and there was nothing to keep her.

Sitting in the car beside him, while Polly shared the back seat with Richard, she wasn't quite sure how she had come to be there. Indeed, she was vague as to which of her two companions had actually invited her to join them, but here she was, prepared to enjoy herself.

It seemed that Professor van Rakesma was prepared to enjoy himself too—answering Polly's excited questions readily, keeping up a relaxed flow of easy talk but never, she noticed, saying a word about himself.

'Where are we going?' asked Polly. She had leaned forward so that her chin was resting on the back of his seat, her safety-belt strained to its limit.

'I thought somewhere by the Thames would be nice. In Oxfordshire.'

'But that's miles away,' said Polly delightedly.

'Not so far, and once we're clear of the suburbs we can use the M4 for a while.' He glanced at Mary. 'Do you know that part of the world?'

'No. Hardly at all. I've been to Oxford——'

'Mary was going to university,' interrupted Polly. 'Only, Mother was ill.'

He asked casually, 'What were you aiming at?'

'English literature and poetry and, if I could manage it, Anglo-Saxon.'

'Well, you are in the right place with Mr Bell.'

'Yes, I'm sure I shall learn a lot with him.'

'What's the use of a lot of stuffy books?' Polly wanted to know. 'You'd be better to get married, Mary.'

'There is always that alternative,' said the professor softly.

She would make some man a good wife, he reflected. Certainly she was an extremely pretty girl, though a bit too stand-offish—perhaps she was shy. He turned his head. 'We turn off here,' he told Polly. 'I do hope you're hungry.'

The Beetle and Wedge was an old ferry inn by the river. Its garden sloped down to the water and there was a restaurant on the houseboat moored at the end. Professor van Rakesma parked the car, secured Richard on his lead, handed him to Polly and went along to see about a table. He had booked earlier and they were shown on to the houseboat, which was already half filled with people lunching.

Mary thanked heaven that she and Polly had dressed with more care than usual; Polly had even been persuaded to abandon her fashionable heavy boots for sandals. As for Mary, she had eased her feet into a pair of high-heeled sandals that she had bought in the January sales and which pinched, although they were the height of fashion.

They were nipping at her toes now, and she wished she could take them off. But she forgot them soon enough as she studied the menu while they drank their cool drinks—no alcohol, of course, since the professor was driving and Polly was too young, but Mary's tonic water with its slice of lemon and tinkling ice was just what she wanted.

The set lunch cost thirty pounds, she noted with concern; she couldn't allow him to pay more than a hundred pounds for the three of them. After all, he was only taking Polly for a drive because she had asked him to.

Perhaps he would have preferred to spend his Sunday with friends, or *a* friend, she thought darkly, frowning at the thought so that he said casually, 'I don't think we'll have the set lunch—may I order for you both? The Dover sole is excellent, and how about garlic mushrooms first and a salad?'

That's better, thought Mary, and turned the page. Dover sole under à la carte was almost as much as the whole of the set lunch. Perhaps if she just asked for a salad... She had no chance; he was ordering, asking Polly if she liked French fries or potato croquettes, and the salad when it came was made up of every rare salad vegetable she could think of.

The mushrooms were delicious, and since she had plenty of common sense she ate them with pleasure and a good appetite. She enjoyed the sole too, with an unselfconscious satisfaction which Professor van Rakesma found charming and a little touching. He hadn't much to say to her, though he joined in Polly's cheerful chatter, pretending not to see that she was slipping some titbit under the table from time to time to a silently waiting Richard.

Mary, eating ice-cream too delicious to describe in normal language, said, 'This is a very beautiful place and the river looks charming. It must be very popular.'

'It is; it's open all the year too, except for Christmas Day. I've been here in winter on a frosty day; it's worth a visit then.'

'Did you come with a young lady?' asked the irrepressible Polly.

He took no notice of Mary's quick, 'Hush, Polly, you mustn't——'

'Indeed I did. She had never been here and she found it very beautiful.'

'Was she beautiful too?' Polly took no notice of Mary's quick breath.

He didn't seem to mind her questions. 'Yes. She doesn't know England very well, so it was a surprise, you see.'

Ah, here she was, thought Mary. The love of his life, and Dutch with it. She wished suddenly that she hadn't come, that she would never see him again, would forget him, meet a man—any man—she thought wildly, who would want to marry her and thus put an end to all this nonsense of loving him.

She concentrated on eating the ice-cream, and when he asked her if she would like coffee replied in a composed voice that she would.

They sat for a while when they had finished their meal, watching the boats on the river, until Mary, on edge that he might want to get back to his home, said that perhaps they should get back. 'Mother and Father will be home by the time we get there,' she added lamely.

It was mortifying to see how readily he agreed, and this time, when Polly asked if she could sit in front, she was only too glad to share the back seat with Richard who, tired out after a short scamper, put his whiskery little head in her lap and went to sleep.

When they reached the house she invited him in in a voice which, while polite, dared him to accept. Professor van Rakesma, being the man he was, accepted. Being shaken off by the ladies of his acquaintance was something he had never experienced before, and it intrigued him.

He sat in the shabby drawing-room, drinking the tea Mary had made and showing no signs of wishing to leave. Filling the kettle for yet more water for the tea, Mary thumped it on to the stove and Bingo, cleaning his whiskers after his supper, gave her an enquiring glance. 'Yes, well, all right,' she said. 'Only I wish he'd go so I never have to see him again.'

She bore the teapot back and Polly handed round second cups and the last of the Maderia cake which Mary had made early that morning. He had two slices. Anyone would think that he hadn't had a good lunch, she reflected; now she would have to make another cake, since everyone else was eating it too.

It was a great pity that he and her father had found something in common—John Donne's poems. The subject lasted them for the best part of an hour until, at length, he said, 'You must forgive me for outstaying my welcome; it is a pleasure to meet someone with the same enthusiasms as oneself.'

Mr Pagett said, 'You must come again; I have one or two rather special books you might like to examine. As for John Donne, we have another enthusiast here—Mary...'

Professor van Rakesma turned to look at her. 'Then
we must certainly renew our acquaintance and share our
opinions,' he said blandly, and watched her go pink. She
muttered something about not having time and he said,
still bland, 'Ah, but one can always find the time for
something one wishes to do.'

'Well, I can't,' said Mary, goaded into rudeness so
that the pink got deeper.

The professor studied her for a moment, and wondered if she knew how lovely she was when she was annoyed. He thought not. Presently he got up to go, making
his farewells with easy good manners, bending his height
so that Polly could kiss his cheek and giving Mary a
smiling nod and a friendly, 'A delightful day, Mary; I
do hope you enjoyed it as much as I did.'

Watching him drive away, she thought that that was
the sort of remark which he could have made equally
well to an aunt or some acquaintance whom he wasn't
likely to see again. Well, he wasn't going to see her again,
was he? Not if she could help it.

Professor van Rakesma, driving himself home, considered his day and, since there was no human companion to listen to his musings, addressed Richard, sitting
beside him. 'Quite pleasant,' he observed. 'In fact I
rather enjoyed myself. Polly is a delightful child; it is a
pity that Mary is so poker-backed.

'I wonder why she is so cautious with me. Do I inspire
you with fright, Richard? Do I behave like an ogre? It
is possible that she just doesn't like me. If I were an
unscrupulous man I might be tempted to do something
about that...! When we first met I found her attractive;
indeed, I went out of my way to get to know her, didn't

I? I wonder why. The instinct to meet a pretty girl again? Possibly.

'I must be warned that she does not share my interest.' He frowned. 'Not that I have any intention of becoming interested.'

To all of which Richard merely rolled his eyes at his master and then went to sleep.

It was after the professor had eaten the dinner that Fred had set before him that he picked up the phone by his chair and dialled a number in Holland.

'Ilsa? Thank you for your letter. I should have answered your other letters, but letter-writing is rather a luxury. I missed you last time I was home—Pleane is coming to stay with me shortly; I wondered if you would care to come with her. You would be company for each other during the day. She wants to do some shopping and you might be able to keep her from being too extravagant.'

'Roel, what a lovely idea! I'd love to come. Could you give me some dates? Perhaps Pleane has it all arranged. I'll go round and see her tomorrow to see if she likes the idea. You're sure I won't be a nuisance?'

He frowned. He had forgotten how sugary-sweet Ilsa's voice was—or perhaps he was comparing it, against his better judgement, with Mary's sensible, unaffected voice. He said quickly, 'Of course not, Ilsa; it will be nice to see you again.' They talked for a few minutes before he rang off with the plea of urgent reports to write.

Not that he did them. He sat in his chair, thinking. It had been a good idea to invite Ilsa. His youngest sister, still in her early twenties, was a darling girl but impulsive; with Ilsa's company she might be induced to get less carried away by whatever caught her fancy at that moment.

As for Ilsa, he had been aware for some time now that
he had only to ask her to marry him to be accepted at
once. She had made her feelings almost embarrassingly
plain on several occasions. And she was, after all, just
the wife he needed—socially acceptable and beautifully
dressed, charming, anxious to please. He would see how
things turned out when she came. They were old friends,
after all; they liked each other, and perhaps liking might
deepen into love or at least affection.

He went upstairs to his bed and dreamed of Mary.

'The girl's getting tiresome,' he told Richard as the
pair of them went for their early morning walk. He
turned his thoughts to planning some kind of enter-
tainment for his two guests when they came, and
presently went off to his consulting-rooms.

Fred, watching him go from his semi-basement
kitchen, wondered out loud what was up. 'Having a lady-
friend, is he?' he asked Richard. 'An old friend, he says.
Thinking of taking a wife, is he? She'd better be an
angel—nothing less is good enough for him. Got his head
in his books half the time and she'll catch him un-
awares.' Fred shook his head. 'I don't like it for an idea,
that I don't.'

Ilsa van Hoeven had put the phone down and gone to
study her face in the enormous mirror on her bedroom
wall. Her reflection smiled back at her and she nodded
approvingly, studying her flawless make-up and elegant
hairstyle. She didn't look her age, thanks to the time
and money she spent on keeping it at bay. She was still
strikingly good-looking, as slim as a wand and always
faultlessly turned out.

And she had made up her mind to marry Roel van
Rakesma. Her first husband had been a mistake; he had

bored her, besides which there had never been enough money. Roel was wealthy, highly thought of in his profession, and had good looks; besides, considering the way he indulged his youngest sister, she would have no trouble in having everything she wanted.

She would go and see Pleane and suggest that she went with her to England for a short visit. She wasn't overfond of the girl, but once she was in Roel's house...

They travelled a week later, and the professor drove to Heathrow to meet their plane. He watched them crossing the reception area, unaware of him, and smiled a little at the sight of Pleane. He was fond of his three sisters but Pleane was his favourite—the youngest, and spoilt, but with a sunny nature and given to doing things on the spur of the moment. It was a pity that he was so busy at the hospital, but Ilsa would keep her company.

He went to meet them then, and Pleane flew into his arms. 'Roel, isn't this fun? There's such a lot I want to do and I must have some new clothes.'

He laughed down at her and turned to Ilsa. 'Nice to see you again, Ilsa.' He sounded friendly but that was all, and although he bent to kiss her too it was merely the social peck—first on one cheek and then the other and then back to the first. It meant nothing and she had to check her irritation; he wasn't a man to demonstrate his feelings in public, and there were ten days ahead of her.

She smiled charmingly at him. 'Nice to see you too, Roel; it seems a long time.'

She hadn't changed, he decided as they went out to the car. She was a woman whom men turned to look at—a woman most men would be delighted to be seen with—so why did he feel no quickening of his pulses? What had he expected? he wondered, and had to admit to himself that he didn't know.

Back at his house, they lunched together before he went back to the hospital. 'I'll be free this evening; if you're not too tired I've tickets for the theatre.'

He forgot all about them once he was sitting in his consulting-room in Outpatients. There were more patients than ever but he worked unhurriedly, giving his attention to each as though he or she were the only one who had come to see him. It was long after five o'clock by the time the last one had gone, and Sister and her nurses began to collect up the papers and forms while he sat on at his desk, making careful notes, phoning and arranging for admissions.

He finished at last and drove himself home; there would be time for him to change, have dinner and get to the theatre.

They were waiting for him, sitting in the drawing-room, and Pleane at least was bubbling over with excitement.

'We thought you'd never get here. I took Richard for a walk to save time.'

'Good girl. Give me fifteen minutes; tell Fred, will you?'

He was as good as his word, joining them in less than that time, immaculate in black tie, looking as though he had had nothing to do all day.

Dinner was enjoyable; Pleane was amusing and happy, and Ilsa took care to be the kind of woman he would like best—serene and pleasant and not drawing attention to herself. A pity, she reflected, that she wasn't young enough to assume an aura of shyness.

They were actually on the point of leaving when Professor van Rakesma was halted by his phone. He took it from his pocket with a glance at his companions and stood listening silently. Presently he said, 'I'll be over in twenty minutes,' and then gave some instructions before he tucked it away again.

'I'll have to go,' he told them. 'But don't worry, I'll get Jim Crosby to go with you. I'll have to take the car but I'll tell him to get a taxi and come here for you. He is my junior registrar and you'll like him.'

He was busy with the phone again as he spoke and then he said, 'He'll be here in ten minutes—he's got rooms five minutes from here.' He looked at them both. 'I'm so sorry.'

'It doesn't matter,' said Pleane at once. 'At least, I'd have liked you to be with us but I'm sure we'll enjoy ourselves.'

'Someone important I expect,' said Ilsa. 'He must be, to call you out at this time of the evening.'

The professor glanced at her. 'An elderly down-and-out found in the park,' he told her evenly. 'And yes, he's important to me as a patient.'

She made a pretty little face. 'Oh, Roel, you're far too important to go out at all hours just for a tramp.' She smiled at him. 'Now, if it had been a member of the royal family... Surely you have registrars and house doctors to see to the hospital patients?'

'Yes, indeed we do. Forgive me if I go. Jim will be here in a few minutes.'

Driving to the hospital, he found himself wondering if Ilsa would be impatient of the interruptions that were bound to occur when they were married. He found that he was thinking of Mary and brushed the thought angrily aside. The girl was becoming a nuisance, popping in and out of his head when he had other and much more important things to think about...

He got home very late and found Fred waiting with hot coffee and sandwiches.

'Can't sleep on an empty stomach,' he said. 'Had a success I hope, sir.'

'I hope so, Fred. Touch and go—he's undernourished and worn out and out of work...'

'Too many of them. He could do with a nice quiet job in the country, I dare say.'

Professor van Rakesma smiled. 'Fred, are you telling me that it would be a good idea if I had a caretaker at the cottage?'

'Well, now you mention it, sir, yes.'

'I'll bear it in mind.' He got up. 'I must be at the hospital by nine o'clock. Breakfast at eight o'clock? I don't know if the ladies will be down.'

'They said they would, but I can take a tray up easy enough.'

Mary found plenty to do now that she was at home again—meals to arrange and cook, washing and ironing, shopping. She enjoyed that now that she could pay for everything, although she had to be very careful how she spent it.

She had seen her father frowning over his post at breakfast. The gas bill, she surmised; the electricity bill would be due soon too, and a few more tiles had fallen off the roof. Luckily they were at the back of the house, where they didn't show easily, but if it rained then one corner of the kitchen would be damp... One thing at a time, she told herself, and sat down at the kitchen table to plan the meals for the days when she wouldn't be there.

Mrs Blackett, coming into the kitchen looking crosser than ever, banged her broom down and flung a duster after it. 'That bathroom tap's leaking something awful; if you don't get a plumber to deal with it soon it'll cost I don't know what.'

Mary said soothingly, 'Yes, I know Mrs Blackett.' The dear soul throve on bad news. 'I'll see about it when I go to the shops presently. Shall we have a cup of tea before you start in here? I'll take one to Mother.'

'Nice to have you at home, darling,' said Mrs Pagett. 'Have you met any nice men at the bookshop?'

'No, Mother; they are mostly elderly and learned, if you see what I mean. Will Father be home for lunch; he didn't say...?'

'It depends, Mary; he was going to see his publishers about something or other. If it's cold it doesn't matter, does it? What are we eating for supper, dear?'

Mary went back presently and drank her cooling tea while Mrs Blackett·grumbled her way through a second cup and half a packet of digestive biscuits. She listened with half an ear to her companion's diatribe concerning the Government and did her anxious sums.

It would work very well, she decided, on her way to work again on Thursday morning; it was a scramble, and there would never be quite enough money, but they would manage until her father's book was finished. Even then they would have to wait for it to be published— months, perhaps—but if she could keep the job everything would come right later on.

She began her day's work under Mr Bell's friendly eye, looking, outwardly at least, perfectly content with her life. She thought of Professor van Rakesma constantly, of course, but since she couldn't help doing that

she did her best to think of him as a passing acquaintance. It didn't always work but she did her best.

Not far away as the crow flew, Pleane and Ilsa were
spending their days shopping. Neither of them lacked
money and they spent it freely, and when they tired of
that they visited art galleries and strolled around St
James's Park while they decided what to do next.

They had enjoyed the theatre, and Pleane at least had
found Jim Crosby very much to her liking. They were
going out to dinner that evening, not just the three of
them, but with several of Roel's friends at the River
Room at the Savoy, and they would dance afterwards.

Ilsa, listening to Pleane's chatter, wondered if she
would be able to get Roel alone. So far she had seen
very little of him—at breakfast, and that was tiresome,
for at home she always breakfasted in bed, and anyway
Pleane chattered unceasingly, and in the evenings—but
never alone.

She had her chance that evening. The dinner had been
most successful; now everyone was dancing, and as they
left the table she said, 'Come on, Roel, the exercise will
do you good.'

He hadn't wanted to dance; he had had a long day
and he would have been content to sit quietly, but good
manners prevailed; besides, she was looking particularly
handsome in the soft lights, and her dress was exquisite.
She gave him a sympathetic little smile. 'You're tired;
how selfish I am. Let's sit here and talk.'

She could be very charming when she wanted, and she
was charming now. She had him to herself for some time
while the others danced. She went to bed that night
well satisfied.

There were still five or six days of their stay left, and she began to plan how she could get him to drive her down to his cottage without Pleane. If she hinted to young Jim Crosby that Pleane would like to see more of the London sights... She went to sleep with a satisfied smile on her face.

She wouldn't have smiled if she had known that Roel was thinking of Mary. Not willingly, though, but somehow it seemed impossible for him to drag his thoughts away from her.

Ilsa was secretly furious when he, in the nicest possible way, told her that it was impossible for him to take her to the cottage. 'I have a consultation on Saturday morning which may well last for some time and possibly take up a good part of the afternoon. Unavoidable, I'm afraid.'

'Well, what about Sunday?' she persisted, pouting prettily. 'I've seen almost nothing of you, Roel, and I'm sure we have a great deal to talk about.'

That was a stupid mistake on her part; Professor van Rakesma, experienced in avoiding various ladies wishing to marry him, said suavely, 'You forget that I promised to take you both to Westminster Abbey on Sunday morning.' He added kindly, for he had known her for a long time, 'We must keep a trip to the cottage for a future date.'

Ilsa, usually so coolly calculating, lost her head. 'We're not going back to Holland till Wednesday. Surely you could spare half a day?'

She contrived to look so wistful that he said with secret reluctance, 'I'll see what I can do; I'm afraid I've been a very poor host.'

She was quick to deny that. 'No, no—we've had a lovely time and I have enjoyed being here in your home.

Fred is splendid, isn't he? Although I think you need a woman here as well.' She trilled with laughter. 'It's a real bachelor establishment, isn't it?'

Her hopes were raised quite erroneously when he said, 'At present, yes.' This time she was wise enough to say nothing more.

It was on Saturday morning that Pleane decided that she wanted to explore. 'We've got all the morning,' she observed. 'I don't want to go to the shops, just poke around. I'll tell Fred that we don't want lunch—we can have it out somewhere. Roel won't be back until the early afternoon. Let's go.'

Ilsa had no wish to explore—she was wearing a new outfit not suitable for showery weather—but it was important for Pleane to like her.

'We could take a taxi,' she suggested.

'I'm sick of taxis; I'd like to walk. You'd better wear some sensible shoes.'

Ilsa had no idea where they were going, but Pleane had. There were people living in cardboard boxes down by the river and she intended to see them for herself. She was impetuous and very extravagant, but she was kind too, always willing to help where help was needed. She had money in her purse and she was bent on giving it away.

It was obvious within a short time that Ilsa wouldn't get far in her high heels; besides, she was sulking. 'We'll take a bus,' said Pleane, oblivious of her companion's ill humour, and boarded one going to Waterloo, standing squashed and happy until they reached the station.

'Down here,' she said breathlessly, and led the way down a dingy side-street.

'Where are you going? You must be mad...'

'I want to see those people I read about who live on the streets—in cardboard boxes, Ilsa, just imagine...'

Ilsa stopped. 'Then if you want to behave like an idiot, go ahead; I'm not coming. I shall go home and have lunch like a decent human being.' She walked away without looking back and Pleane let her go.

CHAPTER SIX

THE clocks were striking five as Professor van Rakesma let himself into the flat. He had been on the point of leaving the hospital earlier in the afternoon but there had been a cardiac arrest in the accident room and he had stayed to do what he could for the man. He wasn't tired, but he was concerned that the man had died despite all his efforts.

Now, as he went in to the hall, he shook himself free from the afternoon's happening; he would take his guests out later on—to dine, perhaps, or to a show if he could get tickets. He was crossing the hall to his study with his bag when Fred joined him. 'You're late, sir; I thought you might have Miss Pleane with you.'

'Pleane? No, she isn't with me, Fred. What has happened?'

'Best talk to Mrs van Hoeven, sir. She's in the drawing-room. I'll bring your tea.'

Ilsa was sitting in one of the comfortable chairs, leafing through a magazine. She had heard Roel come in but she gave a realistic start of surprise as he entered. 'Roel, how late you are. Really, you work too hard; you need someone to make you slow down...'

He had crossed the room to stand by her chair while Richard frisked at his feet. 'Ilsa, where is Pleane? How long has she been away?'

'Oh, so silly, Roel; she wanted to explore so we took a bus to some awful station and started to walk. I said I didn't think it was very interesting, and she said some-

thing about going to see the people who live in cardboard boxes by the river. She absolutely refused to come
back with me.' She shrugged prettily. 'I didn't know what
to do—I mean, what is there to do for such people? And
they are bound to be dirty and diseased.'

'So you came back here?' His voice was quiet.

'Yes. I quite thought she'd come to her senses and be
back by now.' She gave him a sweet smile. 'I'm sure it's
horrid, wherever it is she's gone to—it began to rain and
I had on the wrong shoes...'

'What was the name of the station?'

'Oh, Waterloo. It's not a nice part of London, is it?'

'No, and yet you left Pleane alone there. You'll forgive
me if I go out again.'

'To find her? But you never will—you'll get lost in
all those horrid streets. I'm sure she'll come back when
she's seen all she wants to.'

Professor van Rakesma went to the door. 'Fred will
give you dinner if we're not back.'

Fred was hovering in the hall. 'Going to find her? You
won't want Richard with you, then. I'll have him with
me in the kitchen. I'll serve dinner at the usual time,
shall I, sir? And do be careful.'

'I will, Fred.'

The car was still outside; he got in and drove through
the city until he came to Mr Bell's shop. He went inside
and found it half-full of customers, with Mr Bell perched
on some short steps, handing books down to Mary.

He wasted no time on polite greetings. 'May I borrow
Mary? My sister, Pleane, has taken herself off to some
of the shadier streets by the river—she's been gone for
some hours—and I must find her. It would be easier if
I had someone with me.'

At Mr Bell's nod he looked at Mary. 'You'll come? I need someone sensible and not given to panic.'

It wasn't much of a compliment but she said quietly, 'Yes, of course I'll come, if Mr Bell won't mind.'

'We shall be closing soon, my dear. Run along. Pleane must be found before the evening. Let me know when you find her.'

In the car Professor van Rakesma handed her the phone. 'Perhaps you had better let your family know that you will be late home.'

It was Polly who answered, and he listened with a flash of amusement when Mary said, 'Yes, of course I'm safe; I'm with Professor van Rakesma.' She put the phone back and waited for him to explain.

'Pleane is impulsive—she's a darling girl, wildly extravagant, but she would take the clothes off her back if someone needed them. She has been reading about the homeless who live under the railway arches and along the river—in fact we have talked about it a good deal, but I never realised that she intended to go and see for herself.'

'Is there anyone with her?'

'No. An old friend, Mevrouw van Hoeven, is staying with us, but she returned when they got to Waterloo.' Something in his voice stopped her from asking any more questions.

If the old friend was the woman he intended to marry then of course he wouldn't want her to get involved in what might be, at best, a distressing experience. She said bracingly, 'I've not been in that district, but I should think it would be easy to find her—I mean...' She paused awkwardly. 'Well, she isn't one of them.'

'You're right. She isn't timid, thank heaven. In fact, she's far too friendly—and not always with the right kind of people.'

'She sounds like our Polly. I shan't tell you not to worry, because I expect you're scared stiff, but she hasn't been gone long and we're nearly there. Where will you park the car?'

'Practical Mary. Outside the station—maybe I can find someone to keep an eye on it . . .' He put his 'Doctor on duty' sign on the windscreen and got out. '*You're* wearing sensible shoes . . .'

He went away to talk to a traffic warden on the other side of the road, and she was left to wonder at his remark. The emphasis had been on the 'you're'. She felt a faint prick of resentment at the way he had taken it for granted that they would be sensible.

She was glad of them presently, though. They had walked through narrow, damp streets, with blank-faced warehouses on either side and trains thundering over the bridges above them, and she had had a job to keep up with his long strides, but she managed, sensing that he was too anxious to think of her.

Presently they turned into a labyrinth of dreary streets under more railway arches. Here they found the people who made these places their homes. They were sitting around—some were lying asleep, one or two were eating food from paper bags. The newcomers were watched apathetically until an old woman, surrounded by plastic bags, called out, 'Hi, Doc. You're early and it ain't yer night. There ain't no one ill, either.'

He walked over to her. 'Anne, I am glad to see you on your feet again. I'm looking for my young sister; she came this way earlier today.'

'I see'd 'er. Pretty young miss too. Gorn further down, she 'as. Gave me a few bob too.' She waved an arm in its dirty old coat. 'Yer'll find her.'

He thanked her and walked on, with a silent Mary beside him. So he came here, did he? She knew that teams of doctors and nurses and helpers came each night to do what they could, and her loving heart was filled with pride for him. She didn't speak—this was no time to talk; besides, he was stopping every few yards, asking for his sister.

They had gone quite a long way, passing one or two quarrelsome groups of young men and boys, when Mary said quietly, 'There she is—sitting with those four girls and the boys...'

She couldn't be mistaken; Pleane stuck out like a sore thumb, surrounded by those less fortunate than herself. She had no jacket—it was wrapped around a thin girl sitting beside her—and she was emptying her handbag on to her lap and handing out its contents.

Mary felt Professor van Rakesma's hand grip her arm. 'Yes.' He sounded grim, but as they reached the little group he spoke in a matter-of-fact voice.

'Pleane, I knew we'd find you here.' He sat down beside her and Mary sat on her other side. He glanced round him, smiling. 'Why, it's Elsie, isn't it? How's that sore throat?'

'Doc—didn't recognise you in yer posh clothes.' Elsie looked around at the staring faces. 'Hey, this is Doc; he's all right. Comes 'ere with food and stuff and doesn't preach. Who's the lady, then?'

'This is Mary, a friend of mine.'

There was a general laugh. 'Need a bit of company, did you, Doc?'

They stared at Mary then, and so did Pleane. 'Roel didn't tell me...' she began, and decided not to go on. 'It's been lovely meeting you all,' she said in her fluent, accented English. 'I didn't know Roel came here, but I'm glad I came. If I lived here I'd come with him.' She handed her empty handbag to the nearest girl. 'You have it. I wish I'd brought more money with me; I'd given it all away by the time I got here.'

The professor produced a handful of coins. 'Get some chips or hot drinks. I'll see you next week. Anyone got a job yet?'

There was a chorus of noes.

'Well, don't lose hope—and keep out of mischief!'

Pleane was shaking hands with everyone, and the girl she had given the handbag to kissed her. Amid a chorus of goodbyes they started on their way back, Pleane walking between them. 'You're not angry, Roel? Only, I just had to see for myself—and I was quite safe, you see, and I'm so glad that you come here.' She looked sideways at Mary. 'It was kind of you to come with Roel,' she said shyly.

'Well, I didn't know I was coming,' Mary explained. 'But Professor van Rakesma asked me if I would—it's easier to find someone if there are two of you.'

Pleane gave her a startled look. 'Oh, I thought you were friends...'

'We know each other,' said Mary primly, and didn't see his grin.

'I asked Mary to come with me because she is the only sensible female I know, guaranteed not to lose her head. Sometimes things can be a little tricky down here.'

Indignation swelled Mary's splendid bosom. So that was all she was good for, was it? She had a mind to throw a fit of hysterics there and then, only she wasn't sure how to set about it.

They walked back in silence and got into the car. Professor van Rakesma had taken a quick look at his sister as they reached it and had said mildly, 'Get in the back with Mary, *liefje.*' He looked at his watch. 'I'll take you home first, Mary—Mr Bell will be closed.'

'Thank you. Shouldn't I ring him, though?'

'I'll do that presently.'

The evening traffic was quiet and he drove almost unhindered to Hampstead; Pleane, who had been chattering almost without stopping to draw breath, became silent. As he stopped at Mary's front door she said urgently, 'I'm going to be sick.'

Mary and Professor van Rakesma got out of the car fast and hauled the unfortunate Pleane on to the grass verge—only just in time. 'I feel awful,' said Pleane and fainted.

'Bring her indoors,' said Mary, and ran up the path to fling the door wide. 'Upstairs, the first door on the left.' She went up after him and tossed the quilt aside so that he could lay his sister down. 'You'd better go and lock your car,' she said matter-of-factly. 'I'll get Pleane comfortable.'

Pleane's pretty face was a nasty greenish-white. She opened her eyes as Mary took off her shoes and undid her thin top. 'I feel so awful,' she said, and was sick again just as Professor van Rakesma returned.

Despite his concern for his sister he couldn't help but admire Mary's calm as she bent over Pleane, holding her head and mopping her up in a matter-of-fact way, murmuring soothingly as she did it.

'Did you have anything to eat, Pleane?'

She nodded. 'One of the girls gave me a sandwich. I think it was fish or chicken; it tasted a bit like tin but I was hungry.'

They were speaking in Dutch and he turned to Mary. 'Something she's eaten. The more she vomits the better.' He had brought his bag with him. 'She will be needing fluids...'

'I'll find a nightie for her and get her into bed. I expect you want to look her over. Is there anything you need?'

'No. If I can get her a little better I can drive her home.'

'Nonsense,' said Mary roundly. 'Whatever next? And you a doctor. She can stay here tonight, and if she's better in the morning you can fetch her then. I'll look after her. If I'm worried I shall phone you.'

She turned her head as Polly poked her head round the door. 'What's up? Anything I can do?'

'Yes, love, fetch one of your nighties; Professor van Rakesma's sister isn't feeling very well and is staying here for the night.' She proffered the bowl just at the right moment. 'And please bring a bowl of water and a towel and sponge, will you, and a jug of water?'

'OK.' Polly's head disappeared.

'Your parents will have no objection?' The professor was bending over Pleane, peering down her throat.

'No. They would be upset if you were to take her home while she's feeling so wretched.'

'You're very kind.' He spoke absently. His gentle hands were prodding Pleane's stomach, and he was asking her questions in a quiet voice.

Mary, standing there with a bowl at the ready, reflected that the Dutch language sounded like nonsense. All the same, she wished she could understand what he was saying.

He was saying to his sister that she would be quite safe with Mary—a most sensible girl, not given to panicking. He added, 'I wouldn't leave you here if I wasn't quite sure that I can depend on her.'

Polly came back presently. 'Mother's still in the shed,' she informed Mary, 'and Father's in his study.'

'Good. Be an angel and make some coffee, please, and I expect Professor van Rakesma would like to wash his hands while I get Pleane undressed.'

He went meekly, hiding amusement at Mary's practical manner. Ushered to the bathroom and offered a towel by Polly, he observed, 'Your sister would make a splendid ward sister.'

'Bossy, you mean?' Polly hadn't taken offence. 'You see, she has to look after us and run our house and make a living; she is used to getting things done, otherwise they wouldn't—get done, I mean. She'd really like to be cosseted and cherished and have some time to do what she likes. I'd like her to get married...'

'I'm sure she will marry, Polly; she's very pretty.' He glanced around him and saw the damp patch in the corner, with the bucket underneath it. It would have to be a man with plenty of money, he decided silently. He smiled at Polly and said, 'Shall we go and have another look at the invalid?'

'Is she very ill?'

'I think not. She ate something this afternoon; once she's got rid of it she'll feel better.'

Mary was sitting on the bed, an arm round Pleane, holding the bowl once more, but Pleane looked a little better now. There was a faint colour in her cheeks and Mary had washed her face and hands. When she saw her brother she broke into a torrent of Dutch and he listened gravely.

'Pleane is sorry to cause such a disturbance,' he told Mary. 'You are sure you don't mind her staying here for the night?'

'Of course we don't mind, and she's no trouble at all. I'm going to stay awhile and talk to her while Polly gives you a cup of coffee. Are you hungry?'

He smiled then and she looked away quickly, afraid that he might see how she felt about him. 'Indeed I am— you must be too.'

'That's easy,' said Polly, hovering in the doorway. 'While you have your coffee I'll get some supper. There's heaps left over—bacon and egg pie and there's the rest of the apple tart.' She beamed at him. 'While you and Mary are eating it I'll sit with Pleane, then I can tell you if she's not feeling so good.'

'Splendid, Polly—if Mary doesn't mind.'

'I think it's a very good idea; by the time we've had supper you'll be able to see that your sister's feeling better.'

It was a pity that Pleane chose to be sick again just then; Mary hardly noticed as they went away while she urged her to drink a glass of water.

They came back presently, and Professor van Rakesma pronounced himself satisfied with Pleane's condition. She looked like a wet hen but the worst, he assured her, was over, which left him free to accompany Mary down to the kitchen where she found that Polly had laid a cloth on the kitchen table and set out plates, knives and forks.

'Do sit down,' she urged him. 'It's not very exciting, I'm afraid, but if you're hungry...'

Professor van Rakesma, however, had been taught his manners when a small boy; he didn't sit down until she had served them both, and when they had polished off the bacon and egg pie he gathered up the plates and fetched the apple tart.

'More coffee?' asked Mary, sorry that the meal was over, for surprisingly they had found plenty to talk about.

'That would be nice. Should I perhaps see your father before I go?'

'He'd like that; I'll fetch Mother too. I expect you want to take another look at Pleane.'

'Yes. I think she'll be all right now, but if I may I'll phone about eleven o'clock—that's not too late?'

'No, I'll still be up—and I get up quite early in the morning if you want to phone then.'

'You're very kind.' He sounded formal. 'I'll do that. If you think she is fit I'll fetch her at some time convenient to you.'

She nodded. 'Any time in the morning.' She poured their coffee. 'If you want to ring your home the phone is in the hall. Do use it if you would like to.'

He shook his head and said slowly, 'I have a car phone.'

She said quickly, 'I'll go and tell Father you are here.'

She fetched her mother too and the professor stayed for a short time, saying all the right things in his pleasant voice and presently bidding them goodnight and going upstairs once more to check on Pleane. She was feeling better, but weary from the sickness and spasms of pain. He examined her carefully once more, left tablets for the night, gave Mary a few instructions, bade them all goodnight once again, and went out to his car. Polly went with him.

'You must have had a nasty fright,' she observed.

'Very nasty. Luckily it didn't turn out as badly as it might have done.'

'I like your sister. Is your lady-friend nice too?'

'I don't think I could describe her as that.' He smiled a little but he didn't answer her question. 'I'll be back in the morning. I'm most grateful to Mary.'

'She's super. Such a pity you don't like each other.' She leaned up and gave him a kiss. 'At least, she probably likes you only she pretends she doesn't.'

'Why should she do that?' he asked with interest.

'You can always ask her,' said Polly.

He didn't answer that, but drove himself back home and let himself into the flat. As usual Fred came to meet him in the hall. 'Found Miss Pleane, sir? I was getting a bit worried.'

'Yes, thank you, Fred. She's quite safe, spending the night with someone I know. We found her down by the river...'

'Your pitch?'

'That's right. She appeared to have had a splendid time. Unfortunately she ate some food there and has had a bad tummy upset. I'll fetch her in the morning.'

'You'll be wanting a meal, sir?'

'No, thanks; I had supper at Miss Pagett's home.'

'Very good, sir. Mrs van Hoeven's in the drawing-room.'

'Ah, yes. Thank you, Fred. You gave her some dinner?'

'Yes, sir. I've got Richard in the kitchen with me...'

Professor van Rakesma paused on his way across the hall. 'He can come up now, Fred. I'll take him out presently.'

He opened the drawing-room door and went in.

Ilsa almost ran across the room to him. 'Roel, is she safe? You have no idea how awful I feel—I never thought she would go off like that—she knew that I didn't want to go through those filthy little streets.'

He didn't sit down but went to the French window leading to the small garden behind the flats, opened it and let Richard out. 'Yes, I found her, Ilsa. She's spending the night with some people I know.'

He didn't say any more and Ilsa, sensing that he wasn't going to tell her anything further, wisely said nothing for a while. Presently she said, 'You do forgive me, Roel? It was stupid of me; I should have remembered that Pleane is so impulsive.'

When he didn't answer she asked, 'These people that she's with—they'll take good care of her? Could you not have brought her here? She's not ill?' She gave a little shudder. 'Not caught something frightful from those people she met?'

'She is very tired. She walked a long way; she will be quite herself after a good night's sleep. I shall fetch her tomorrow morning.'

'I'll come with you; it's the least I can do...' She smiled at him, unable to read the expression on his face. Amusement? Amazement?

She was a conceited woman; she had no idea that it was well-concealed contempt.

Mary, pottering around in her dressing-gown, wishful to go to bed but waiting for the professor's phone call, had ample time to reflect upon the evening's happenings.

She was still smarting from the knowledge that he considered her a sensible female. On the other hand she was agreeably surprised to discover that he went out at night to help the hapless men and women who were homeless; what was more, she doubted if anyone knew about it.

Under his impersonal courtesy there must be a rather nice man lurking. He had sat down with that grubby, ill-cared for group of young people as though he made a habit of it. Perhaps he did. He had been nice about his sister going off like that too...

The phone rang and she hurried to answer it, fearful of waking everyone up, which was perhaps why she sounded brisk and a little impatient.

'Got you out of bed, Mary? My apologies. Is Pleane asleep?'

'Yes, I've just been in to see her. She hasn't been sick again and she feels quite cool. I'm in the room next door. I'll hear her if she wakes up.'

'Good. If she wants breakfast in the morning she can have it, but will you take her temperature first? I'll be with you about eleven o'clock, if that's convenient.'

'Quite convenient, Professor van Rakesma. I'll look after her. Goodnight.'

She hung up quickly, suddenly not wanting to talk to him, and went to bed—to wake several times during the night and peer at the sleeping Pleane.

In the morning she had just escorted her to the bathroom, where she had run a steaming hot bath for her—which meant that the water would be lukewarm for the rest of the day—when Polly came racing upstairs.

'He's here and there's someone with him. A lady—ever so smart and all smiles. I don't like her. She looked at me as though I was wearing all the wrong clothes.'

Mary eyed her sister. 'Well, love, I know you're wearing what everyone else your age is wearing at the moment, but perhaps she finds it a bit strange. Go down and get the coffee, will you? It's all ready in the kitchen. And make sure that Mother or Father—both, if you can find them—are there. I'll tell Pleane; she'll be so pleased.'

Pleane wasn't pleased. 'Ilsa's there? But I do not wish to be with her. She is not what you call a sport; she ran away yesterday because she wears high heels and is afraid to get dirty. I can see that she wants very much to marry Roel, and that will not do.'

She got out of the bath and wrapped herself in the towel Mary offered her. 'Now, you would do very well for him, but I think you might not agree; you are not friends, you said yesterday, and I find that strange since you came with him to find me.'

Mary reflected on the perversity of people. Polly had seen her as a suitable wife for Professor van Rakesma, and now here was his sister of like mind, while he thought of her—if he did think at all—as sensible, with her head screwed on straight. She gave a delicate shudder and offered to dry Pleane's back.

'I've done the best I could with that stain on your dress,' she observed. 'I'm not sure what it was, and I don't think I want to know, but I expect if you take it to a good cleaner's they'll get it out.'

'Oh, I'll throw it away. Roel will buy me another one.' Pleane was dressing quickly. 'We were to have gone to church this morning. We are going home on Wednesday and I did want to go to Westminster Abbey.'

'You could go to evensong.'

'Yes? You go to this evensong?'

'Sometimes, but usually we all go in the morning.'

'And you couldn't go this morning because I am here. I'm so sorry.'

'Don't worry; we were going this evening anyway.'

'I wish I could come with you.'

'We'd love to have you, but I expect your brother has other plans.'

Pleane said nothing more, and presently they went downstairs to the drawing-room to find Ilsa talking to her parents. There was no sign of the professor.

Pleane shook hands with Mr and Mrs Pagett, said hello to Ilsa and introduced her to Mary. 'Ilsa's a friend of my mother's,' she explained, and Mary hid a smile at the indignation on Ilsa's face. After all, she wasn't all that old.

She exchanged various civilities and, saying that she would fetch the coffee, went to the kitchen. Polly was there, carefully pouring the coffee while Professor van Rakesma leaned against the table, eating one of the cakes that Mary had made that morning.

His good morning was genial. 'I must apologise for spoiling your Sunday morning and bringing Ilsa with me; she was so anxious to see that Pleane was quite well again.' Something in his voice made her look sharply at him, and he met her eyes with a guileless stare. 'You have all been so kind.'

He carried the tray in and Polly took the cakes; Mary stayed behind in the kitchen for a few minutes, mumbling an excuse about more coffee, but really it was because she didn't want to see him with this Ilsa woman. Who had disliked her on sight. Mary took several heartening breaths and went to join everyone else.

Ilsa was sitting on the edge of the little Victorian balloon-backed chair which needed a new cover so badly; she gave the impression of being uncomfortable while behaving with impeccable good manners. She refused a cake with a sweetly rueful smile. 'I have to be so careful of sweet food,' she explained.

Mary, biting into her own cake, murmured with false sympathy. 'There's so much of me that it doesn't matter what I eat,' she said cheerfully, and Professor van Rakesma, listening to her mother explaining about her greetings cards, turned a laugh into a cough and agreed pleasantly that robins at Christmas-time were always popular.

Ilsa was on edge to go, but neither he nor Pleane were to be hurried. Richard had come with them and was sitting by his master, gobbling any oddments of cake which came his way, and providing a topic of conversation.

Mrs Pagett, free from her daughter's inhibitions, plied her guest with questions—was he married? No? Then he ought to be. Had he a family in Holland? Yes? And where did they live, and were any of them married? How many were there and how often did he go back to his home there? Did he intend to live in England forever?

Mary, making polite small talk with an impatient Ilsa, listened to his answers and stored them away for future reflection.

The two men went away presently, to look at some manuscripts of her father's, and they didn't return for half an hour or more, by which time Ilsa was white with bottled-up annoyance. Her goodbyes, when at last Professor van Rakesma observed that they really should be going, were uttered in a voice cold enough to cause even gentle, whimsical Mrs Pagett some astonishment, but nothing could have been warmer than Pleane's thanks and her brother's firm handshake.

He didn't shake Mary's hand, though; he thanked her formally for her help and made no reference to their meeting again.

'Oh, well,' said Mary, shutting the door firmly as he drove away. 'That's that.'

The rest of the day stretched tamely ahead of her now that he had gone. She banged about in the kitchen, preparing the Sunday joint, and wished that he wasn't so tiresome, turning up just when she was schooling herself to think no more of him.

She and Polly went for a walk that afternoon, and after tea accompanied their parents to church. Evensong was Mary's favourite service; she sang the hymns with pleasure in her clear voice and felt better—until she turned her head cautiously to see who was singing with equal enthusiasm only in a deep, rumbling voice. Professor van Rakesma, no less, with Pleane on one side of him and Ilsa on the other.

Mary turned her head quickly, but not quickly enough, so that she had time to note that Ilsa was wearing a striking outfit and a most becoming hat. She sat through the sermon, not hearing a word of it, wondering why he and his companions should be there, but it wasn't until they were leaving the church that her father observed, 'Ah, I see that our guests have come.' And when Mary looked at him enquiringly, he added, 'I'm sure that you will give them one of your delicious meals, my dear.'

'Delicious meal—when, Father?'

'Why, presently, Mary; I invited them for supper. Professor van Rakesma and I have a mutual interest in the history of mid-Europe; it will be a splendid opportunity for him to examine several books that I have...'

Mary reminded herself that she loved her father deeply, thrust aside any unfilial thoughts which crowded into her head and concentrated on supper as they moved slowly towards the church porch.

Professor van Rakesma, Ilsa and Pleane were there, talking to the vicar and her mother and Polly, and they joined them, exchanged a few words with the vicar and began to walk slowly out of the churchyard.

Mary had greeted everyone politely, avoided Polly's eloquent eye and engaged Ilsa in conversation. Her remarks received short shrift and it was a relief when her mother and father were invited to get into the car with Pleane and Ilsa and be driven the short distance home, which left Mary and Polly free to tear through several short cuts and get there at the same time.

Everyone went into the drawing-room, where Mr Pagett offered sherry, and afterwards Mary slid away to the kitchen to poke her head into the fridge and the larder and look at the remains of the joint, a wedge of cheese and, thankfully, bacon and eggs. They would have to wait at least half an hour, she thought, rapidly gathering what she would need for a bacon and cheese quiche.

While the oven heated she made the pastry. 'And if it turns out like lead they'll just have to eat it,' she told Bingo, who was watching her from his chair. The bacon fried and the eggs beaten, she almost flung them into the pastry case and banged the oven door on it.

'They'll have to eat a salad,' she informed him. 'Thank heaven there are some lettuces in the garden.' She thumped her gleanings from the vegetable rack on to the table and turned round to see Professor van Rakesma standing just behind her. 'Now what do you want?' she asked him crossly. 'Of all the tiresome men...'

He said gravely, his lids lowered over amused eyes, 'I fear we have put you out. I will make some excuse and we can go in a few minutes.'

'Oh, no, you don't! I've just put a quiche in the oven; you'll jolly well stay and eat it.'

'If you say so. Shall I fetch some lettuce from the garden?'

She was chopping tomatoes, grating carrots and slicing beetroot. 'Yes—no, you'd better not. You'll get your hands dirty.'

'It wouldn't be the first time.' He wandered out of the kitchen door and presently returned with two lettuces which he put in the sink. 'Mary, I'm sorry about this; I had no idea that you knew nothing about it. Your father invited us and I took it for granted that you would know. Pleane very much wanted to go to evensong and he knew that.'

'Yes, well...I was very rude to you just now; I apologise, but you see we don't entertain any more and there's not much in the fridge.'

'I'm sure we shall enjoy our supper, whatever it is. Shall I lay the table?'

'Lay the table? You? But I don't suppose you know how—I mean...' She frowned. 'You know very well what I mean.'

'Try me and see. Here or in the dining-room?'

'Oh, not here, not with——' She stopped just in time. 'In the dining-room, and thank you. Everything you'll need is in the dresser over there.'

CHAPTER SEVEN

PROFESSOR VAN RAKESMA, put on his mettle, laid the table with a precision and nicety which would have earned Fred's praise, and, that done, he wandered back into the kitchen, where Mary was setting out the biscuits and cheese.

'Don't you want to go to the drawing-room? Father said there were some books...'

'Presently, I fancy. I left him enjoying a talk with Ilsa.'

The silence went on rather too long. 'She's very handsome,' said Mary, 'and that was a lovely hat. I hope she doesn't find us too dull.'

He didn't answer, which was annoying of him; she cast around for something else to talk about, since he obviously had no intention of going. 'I expect your sister is enjoying herself——' that was rather a silly remark to make after yesterday's adventure '—shopping and so on,' she went on lamely.

'Don't try so hard, Mary,' he said. 'We may not be friends, but we know each other well enough by now to be able to cut out the small talk.' He glanced at her. 'And now I have annoyed you.'

'Anything you say is of complete indifference to me,' said Mary grandly, and tightened her hand on the wooden spoon that she was holding.

He laughed then, and threw up his hands. 'I cry *pax*; shall we bury the hatchet until we meet again?'

'Certainly, but we aren't likely to meet any more.'

'Don't tempt fate.'

'Pooh,' said Mary, and took the quiche out of the oven.

To her surprise supper was a success. The conversation never flagged, composed as it was largely of Christmas robins, first editions, and, on a more serious note, the homeless Pleane had met, and although Professor van Rakesma spoke with some authority on the subject he didn't mention that he went down regularly to the riverside shelters.

Only Ilsa was silent for most of the time, pushing her supper round her plate in a well-bred fashion, brightening up when the professor spoke to her, smiling at him in a sweetly understanding manner which set Mary's splendid teeth on edge.

Once the meal was finished, her father bore his guest away to his study and her mother led Ilsa back to the drawing-room to listen in her vague, kind way to her view on a number of subjects.

'Of course,' she declared, 'I shall dismiss Fred; I don't approve of manservants. A good housekeeper and daily help is quite enough at Roel's flat. It's large, but it is easily run.' She gave Mrs Pagett a wistful smile. 'Of course, I'm quite hopeless at anything to do with housework.'

'Oh, so am I,' agreed Mrs Pagett cheerfully. 'Such a waste of time, I always think, and Mary is such a splendid manager; I'm sure I don't know what we would do without her. You intend to marry?'

Ilsa turned an earnest face to her. 'Oh, most certainly, Mrs Pagett.'

Mrs Pagett, who wasn't always as vague as she appeared to be, thought of the look she had surprised on her elder daughter's face when she had glanced at the professor and felt a pang of grief for her. They would have made a splendid pair; if only he had fallen in love with Mary instead of this hard-faced woman sitting opposite her. She said conventionally, 'I'm sure you will be very happy.' And, since she was a kind woman, added, 'It must have been sad to lose your husband.'

'Oh, I divorced him. He didn't understand me and he bored me. He was so serious, and I believe that one should enjoy life. I like theatres and dancing and lovely clothes.' She gave a little trill of laughter. 'And lots of money. But we all do, don't we?'

Mrs Pagett agreed quietly, reflecting that from what she had seen of Professor van Rakesma he didn't appear to be any less serious than Ilsa's former husband. Perhaps being in love would alter him.

He came into the room with her own husband then, and she could see that Ilsa was sadly mistaken in her wish to change him. Here was a man who might fulfil his social obligations with charm and good manners, but they had no chance against his work as a doctor. She watched Ilsa turn to him with a charming smile.

'Roel, I've had such a lovely evening, but perhaps we should take our leave.' She glanced at her watch and gave a start of surprise. 'It's almost ten o'clock.'

He made no demur, and when Mary and Polly came into the room goodbyes were said and Pleane, who had been in the kitchen with them, declared that she would see them before she went back to Holland. 'I wish you lived nearer,' she said, 'but next time I come you must come and stay with us. There's heaps of room in Roel's flat.'

If her brother heard this invitation he gave no sign, but Mary saw Ilsa's angry glance. She said loudly, 'We would like that very much,' and was kissed three times, continental-fashion, by Pleane. Ilsa shook hands and Professor van Rakesma gave her a cool nod.

'What a very nice man,' observed Mrs Pagett as they went back to the drawing-room. 'And so is his sister—but I don't much care for his friend; she didn't much care for us, did she?'

'No, Mother, but I expect she leads rather a different life from ours. You know, clothes and hairdressers and beauty parlours and a busy social life.'

With a sudden flash of waspishness her mother said, 'She must be looking forty in the face. Perfect make-up of course, but I could see the wrinkles.'

Mary gave her mother a hug. 'Mother, how unkind,' she said, and laughed. 'Why didn't you like her?'

'She said that painting greetings cards was childish.' Mrs Pagett frowned. 'She said several things that made me want to shake her.'

'Well, it's a good thing that we shan't see her again. Are you going to bed? Or shall we make a list of shopping for tomorrow?'

Breakfast was just finished when an enormous floral arrangement was delivered to Mrs Pagett. She opened the little envelope tucked in among the roses and lilies and read it out loud. '"Thanking you for your kind hospitality"——' She looked up. 'I can't read the signature; it's dreadful writing...'

'"R van R",' said Mary. 'How kind of him. Where do you want them, Mother?'

'Where we can all see them; I'll find a place while you are shopping.'

On Tuesday morning, just as Mary and Mrs Blackett were sitting down for their mid-morning cup of tea, Pleane and Ilsa arrived. Mrs Blackett had gone to answer the doorbell—not because she felt it her duty to do so but because she wanted to see who it was. She came back into the kitchen and sat down again. 'Two ladies. Want to see you, Miss Mary. Very posh.'

'Someone collecting for the church?' hazarded Mary. 'Where is my purse?'

Pleane and Ilsa stood in the hall and she was instantly vexed that she was in an elderly cotton dress with the sleeves rolled up, and, worse, her hair lay in a thick plait over one shoulder.

Pleane didn't appear to notice; she went to meet her with a wide grin. 'I know we're a nuisance, but I did want to say goodbye once more. We're off early tomorrow—everything's packed...' She looked down at her elegant person. 'That's why we are all dressed up.'

'Will you have a cup of coffee?' asked Mary, and Ilsa answered before Pleane could speak.

'How kind, but we wouldn't dream of interrupting your housework—the taxi is outside waiting. We have to go to Fortnum & Mason for my mother's special brand of tea; we can have coffee there.'

Mary spent a moment wondering if Ilsa's mother was as unpleasant as her daughter. 'A long way just to get some tea...'

'Ah, but we usually have it sent, you know. But since I am here it seemed a good idea to get it and take it back with me. Pleane, are you coming?'

Pleane had an expression on her face which reminded Mary of her brother—a bland look which gave nothing away. 'I am just going to see Mrs Pagett—I didn't say goodbye to her properly.' She smiled at Mary. 'Is she in the shed?'

'Yes, but I'm sure she'd love to see you again. Would you like to go too, Ilsa?'

'No, no. I'll wait in the taxi.' She watched Pleane go through the drawing-room doors into the garden and then turned to look at Mary; the look started at her bare feet in their shabby sandals and moved slowly up to her face. She smiled then, but her eyes were like blue glass. 'Walk down to the gate with me if you can spare the time; I'm sure Pleane won't be long.'

So they walked down the short, neglected drive, Ilsa stepping carefully in her high-heeled shoes. Mary choked back a wish for her to trip up and fall flat on her face, dislodging the elegant hat and dirtying the deceptively simple outfit she was wearing, but of course she didn't.

It wasn't until they reached the open gate that she spoke. 'We must come and see you again,' she said. 'I shall be back very shortly; there is so much to do—the flat needs new covers and curtains and I shall change the colour scheme. I must persuade Roel to get rid of Fred too; I was telling your mother—a good house-keeper and a daily woman must take over.' She laughed a little. 'Men are so useless at that kind of thing, aren't they? Or perhaps you wouldn't know.'

Mary was leaning on the gate; her plait had fallen over her shoulder and half hid her face. She said, 'No, I wouldn't know. You're going to make rather drastic changes, are you not?'

'Very drastic—and not just in the flat. I shall see to it that Roel's life is changed too. A social life is so important.'

'You're going to be married?' Mary managed to ask the question lightly.

'My dear girl, isn't it obvious?'

'No...'

'Well, of course, if one is influenced by one's feelings, even when they are mistaken...'

Mary turned her lovely brown eyes on Ilsa's smiling face. 'I'm glad we shan't meet again,' she said clearly. 'Here's Pleane.' She turned her back on Ilsa and went to meet the other girl.

'Your mother is a darling—almost as nice as mine, Mary. Ilsa, you look as though you're sucking a lemon; it makes you look quite old.'

She kissed Mary and went out to the taxi and Ilsa, without speaking again, followed her.

Back in the kitchen Mary added boiling water to the teapot and sat down at the table.

'Well?' said Mrs Blackett, all agog. 'Oo was it, then?'

'The doctor who looked after Great Aunt Thirza—it was his sister. And the lady with her says she is going to marry him.'

'Oh, yes? There's many a slip, I always say. That was the tall one with the made-up face? Can't say I took a liking for 'er.'

'Neither did I. She was going to Fortnum & Mason to order a special brand of tea for her mother.'

Mrs Blackett gave a guffaw. 'Very la-di-da, and what's wrong with teabags, I'd like to know?' She took her mug to the sink. 'I'll go and give that dining-room table a bit of a polish before I clean up 'ere.'

Mary drank her tea, made a cup of coffee for her mother and went down to the shed.

'That nice girl came to see me,' observed the older woman happily. 'Such a chatterbox too...'

'Mother,' said Mary, 'did Ilsa tell you that she was going to marry Professor van Rakesma?'

'Ah, she was here too, was she? As a matter of fact, not in so many words but as good as, if you see what I mean. All that talk about changing his home and getting rid of someone called Fred—his manservant, presumably. She'll make him a bad wife; the man must be out of his mind.'

Mary said tartly, 'Presumably at his age he knows his own mind well enough.'

'Yes, that's why I'm rather surprised. He didn't behave as though he loved her, did he? His manners are so good it was hard to tell. He's not one to wear his heart on his sleeve, is he?'

'I have no idea, Mother.'

'You sound as though you don't like him, love.'

'I don't know him well enough to say one way or the other. I hope he'll be happy with Ilsa.'

Two fibs in one breath.

Mrs Pagett murmured, 'Of course, dear. What a delicious cup of coffee.'

Professor van Rakesma had rearranged his visits and consultations so that he could see his sister and Ilsa on to their early morning plane. He was going out of his door with Richard for their morning walk when Pleane came racing downstairs. 'I'm coming with you,' she told him, and slipped a hand under his arm. 'I want to talk.'

He looked down at her with affection. 'Do you ever want to do anything else? What have you done now? Fallen in love again?'

'No, no, it's not me this time—it's you. You and Ilsa.'

'And what about us? Something I should know?'

He was half laughing and she said quickly, 'No, don't laugh. Do you like her very much, Roel?' And at his quick frown she said, 'No, don't be cross—and I'm serious. Don't tell me it's none of my business.'

'Very well, I won't. Have you quarrelled with her, *liefje*?'

'No. I never liked her very much, you know, but she comes to see us a lot and says she's our oldest friend—that kind of thing—and she bosses me around. But it's not that. She's going to marry you—did you know?'

'I have sometimes wondered if she had that in mind.'

'Don't, will you? She's all wrong for you, Roel. You need a wife like Mary Pagett, who'll stand up to you and not waste your money, and will have hordes of children for you.'

He squeezed her hand and said kindly, 'Pleane, Mary and I are almost always at daggers drawn...'

'Except when you want someone to help you—like when you came looking for me.'

'That was the exception which proves the rule. No, my dear, I'm afraid that wouldn't be a very good idea. But if it will relieve your mind I promise you that I don't intend to marry Ilsa; indeed I have no plans to marry at the moment.'

With that Pleane had to be content; if Roel said he wasn't going to marry Ilsa then everything was all right; he was a man of his word.

She would have been relieved if she had known that he had been shocked at Ilsa's light-hearted attitude to Pleane's escapade. Until then he hadn't realised how selfish she was, and how uncaring of things which touched on her comfort or peace of mind. Any ideas of marrying her which he had been harbouring at the back of his mind had been swept away.

He stayed with them until it was time for them to board their plane, bade them goodbye, gave Pleane a final hug, and then drove himself back to his home.

'Got half an hour?' asked Fred, coming into the hall, duster in hand. 'I've a pot of coffee all ready for you.'

'Splendid, Fred. I'd like it now—I'll be in the study.'

Fred came in presently, poured the coffee and stood waiting by the desk.

Professor van Rakesma looked up from the notes he was studying. 'Fred?'

'It's like this, sir. Mrs van Hoeven told me that she won't want me no more when she comes; so what's me and Syl going to do?'

The professor sat back in his chair. 'As far as I know, Fred, Mrs van Hoeven won't be coming here again; perhaps there has been some misunderstanding, for we are certainly not going to marry.' He smiled suddenly. 'And, when I do marry, I can promise you that you and Syl will stay with us for as long as you wish to—and I hope that will be for a very long time.'

'Thank you, sir. It had us a bit worried.'

It had the professor a bit worried too; he had never, to the best of his knowledge, led Ilsa to believe that he intended to marry her, although he knew that if he had done so she would have accepted at once. He would have to make it plain to her next time they met. If he could find someone whom he would want for his wife it would make things so much easier...

Mary's face flashed beneath his lids and he dismissed it at once; they struck sparks off each other whenever they met and she made no bones about her indifference to him. But then, of course, he reminded himself, he was indifferent to her too.

He returned to his case-notes and forgot about her, for the time being at least.

He didn't get home again until the early evening. He had had several private patients to see at his rooms in Harley Street, and from there he had gone straight to the hospital to do a ward round. The man he had been called to see on the day of Pleane and Ilsa's arrival was getting on well, and he pondered the idea of offering him the job of caretaker at his cottage at Adlescombe.

The man had no family and no friends and, being homeless, had been unable to get a job for lack of references and an address. He could take him on for a month and see if he was suitable. He was a quiet man, who had seen better days and would never be fit for heavy work again, but there was little to do at the cottage.

He was still thinking about it when Pleane phoned to say that they were home again and to thank him for her holiday. 'And all those lovely clothes.' She added, 'Ilsa went home; she said she'd phone you from there.'

Ilsa did ring later that evening, but it was Fred who answered her, to tell her with well-concealed satisfaction that Professor van Rakesma had been called back to the hospital to an emergency and he had no idea when he would be back.

She hung up without leaving a message and Fred went back to the kitchen to tell Richard that she wasn't half put out. 'You didn't like her, neither,' said Fred. 'Doesn't like dogs nor cats. I don't call that natural.' Richard, an intelligent beast, didn't call it natural either.

Mary attacked the housework with even more vigour than usual after her conversation with Ilsa; she refused to admit, even to herself, that the idea of never seeing the professor again made her feel quite ill, and as for his marrying Ilsa... Her mind boggled at the very idea.

'A pity I shall not be seeing him again,' she told Bingo—a sentiment, if she had but known it, which was shared by Professor van Rakesma, albeit reluctantly.

She welcomed her return to the bookshop on Thursday. A change of scene, she told herself, would soon put things in their proper perspective. And certainly she was busy enough to preclude any sitting about being sorry for herself.

It was going on for six o'clock on Saturday afternoon when he came into the shop. It was already crowded, and his bulk meant that everyone was standing almost shoulder to shoulder. Mary, wreathing her substantial person through the throng, intent on brown paper and string, ran full tilt into him.

He put an arm round her to steady her, but only for a moment. 'Doing good business, I see. Any chance of seeing Mr Bell?'

'He's in his office.'

He nodded. 'I'll drive you home.'

'There's no need, thank you all the same; the underground is very quick.'

'Don't be childish, Mary. You know as well as I do that it's much more comfortable for you if I drive you there. And no sneaking out of the back door...' He had gone before the peevish words on her tongue could be uttered.

There was no sign of him when she ushered the last customer out of the door, and there was no sound of voices coming from Mr Bell's office. Perhaps he had had second thoughts. Despite her resolve not to go with him she felt disappointed; she would have enjoyed re-iterating her refusal, she told herself firmly, and put her head round the office door.

Mr Bell was there, deep in a book, and, sitting on the other side of his desk, was Professor van Rakesma, his commanding nose buried in a little leather-bound book, which she recognised as one of Mr Bell's choicest first editions.

She said quickly, 'Goodnight, Mr Bell,' nodded in the professor's general direction and closed the door gently.

Not smartly enough. She had reached the shop door when his hand came down on hers, about to turn the knob. 'I'm not coming with you,' she said as he swept her across the pavement, round the corner and into the car before she could draw breath.

Richard was asleep on the back seat, but he got up to greet her as she settled in her seat with what dignity she had left. 'I cannot think,' she began, 'why you persist in annoying me, Professor van Rakesma.'

'I am not sure myself,' he told her mildly. 'You are a perpetual thorn in my otherwise disciplined life.' He turned to look at her. 'To mix my metaphors, you are like a sore tooth that I'm unable to leave alone.'

Her brown eyes flashed with temper. 'Well, a thorn, indeed, a sore tooth—whatever next, I should like to know?'

'I've been wondering that myself. Do you suppose we might cry quits and become friends?'

Friends, thought Mary wildly. Who wants to be friends? And he's almost a married man. 'Certainly not.'

'You don't like me?'

He had begun to drive towards Hampstead.

'I didn't say that.'

'Good. In that case let us at least assume an armed neutrality. I need your help.'

'Mine? Whatever for?'

'Well, if I may tell you... I have a cottage in Gloucestershire at Adlescombe near Stow-on-the-Wold. I go there for weekends occasionally, and when I can manage a few days off. I have decided to have a caretaker there but I think there are one or two improvements which should be made—the kitchen and so forth—before he takes up his residence. It needs a woman's eye, though. If Pleane had been staying longer I would have got her to go with me. I'm free tomorrow if you would be kind enough to give me the benefit of your advice.'

'What sort of improvements?' asked Mary cautiously.

'I'm not sure; that's why I'm asking you to come and see for yourself and tell me.' He gave her a sideways glance. 'That is all I'm asking, Mary.'

She didn't allow her thoughts to dwell on the enchanting prospect of spending a whole day with him; she would remember to be friendly in a detached way, bearing in mind all the time that he was going to marry the hateful Ilsa and taking care not to ask questions. Of course, if she were Ilsa she would never allow him to spend the whole day with another girl, however business-like the intentions were. She must feel very sure of him...

'Yes, I'd like to come, thank you! Is your cottage quite empty? I mean, does someone go in now and then and dust around and make sure everything's safe?'

'Yes, Mrs Goodbody from the village "pops in"—those are her words—now and then. I've no idea what she does; there doesn't seem much point in dusting if there is no one there. It all looks perfectly all right when I go.'

Of course, when he was married to Ilsa it would be a good idea to have someone there to keep the place in a state of readiness. She couldn't imagine Ilsa putting on an apron and peeling the potatoes.

'I'll call for you around half-past nine—if that's not too early for you?'

'I'll be ready. Do you want me to bring some food—sandwiches and so on?'

'Fred will see to that. I shall bring Richard with me.'

'Oh, good. I expect he likes the country.'

He drew up outside the house and got out to open her door.

'Would you like to come in and have some coffee?'

She hoped that he would say no while at the same time not wanting him to drive away. All the same, when he refused politely she felt let down.

'Thank you for the lift,' she said then, anxious not to keep him—perhaps he was going out that evening. 'I'll be ready in the morning. Goodnight.'

He smiled, and got into the car and drove away and she stood on the doorstep and watched him go.

Spending the day with him would mean some re-organisation of Sunday.

Polly, when told the news, volunteered at once to see to lunch. 'As long as you leave everything ready to put in the oven. You'll be home for supper, won't you?'

'Gracious, yes. By teatime, I should think. I'd better make a few of those little cakes. I'll go and talk to Mother. Is she in the hut?'

'Yes. Father's over at the vicarage.'

Mary was up early to find the sky overcast, which was in a way a good thing because she could wear the green cotton jersey dress—which was about the nicest one she had—without looking too warmly clad.

Breakfast was over and everything left in apple-pie order by the time Professor van Rakesma thumped the doorknocker. He was admitted and then spent ten minutes or so chatting to her mother and father.

He looked calmly self-assured, utterly to be trusted and pleasantly detached in his manner—all of which pleased Mrs Pagett, which was what he had intended.

Polly, running round the garden with Richard, thought once again that it was a pity that Mary and he couldn't get married. He'd be a splendid brother-in-law.

He took the M40 out of London. Traffic was light and the Rolls ate up the miles in a well-bred silence while they talked in a desultory fashion about nothing much, bypassing High Wycombe and then Oxford and finally stopping in Burford at the Lamb Inn for coffee and to allow Richard to stretch his legs. The village was charming and very peaceful, and they walked for ten minutes or so, content to be silent in each other's company.

They turned on to the road to Stow-on-the-Wold presently and then to Adlescombe, a village of no great size with houses built of yellow Cotswold stone—most of them cottages around the church. Professor van Rakesma drove down the narrow main street and into a short, gateless drive.

The cottage was bigger than its neighbours, with small, latticed windows, a solid front door with a little porch, and dormer windows in a slate roof which was old and moss-covered in places. There was a nice arrangement of shrubs and flowers all around.

A delightful little house, thought Mary, very much aware of his great arm flung around her shoulders as he helped her out of the car.

'You must want to come here very often.'

'Yes. It's delightful, isn't it? Come inside.'

He unlocked the door and she went past him into a small lobby and then into the room beyond, which was low-ceilinged and beamed, with an inglenook and windows at both ends of the room. The furniture was exactly right—oak and simple, with comfortable easy chairs and two vast sofas on either side of the fireplace. The floor was wooden, worn by the years and covered with several lovely, slightly shabby rugs. There was dust on the gateleg table by the far window, although everything was tidy and clean.

'A good polish,' said Mary, and Professor van Rakesma gave a shout of laughter.

'But you like it?'

'It's exactly right.'

She looked questioningly at him and he said easily, 'I spent a long time getting exactly what I wanted to furnish the cottage. Some of the furniture I brought back from

Holland.' He opened a latched door. 'Come and look at the kitchen.'

It was small and rather bleak. There was an Aga against one wall, and cupboards and shelves, an old porcelain sink and a solid table with Windsor chairs. There was everything there but no colour.

'Pale yellow walls, rush matting, a picture or two, and another shade on the light.'

There was an old-fashioned dresser opposite the Aga. There were plates and cups and saucers on it, obviously bought without any thought of a colour scheme. 'Orange and blue,' said Mary. 'Glasses and jugs—and flowers, of course.'

'Of course,' agreed Professor van Rakesma gravely. 'Come and see the dining-room.'

It was a small room, with exactly the right wallpaper, a round mahogany table with four chairs round it, and a Georgian sideboard with nothing on it. The curtains were chintz, the same as those in the sitting-room, and there were cushions piled on the window-seat. There were a few paintings on the walls—gentle landscapes, nicely framed.

'Perfect,' sighed Mary, and followed him through the narrow door in one wall, behind which were narrow stairs. They led to a roomy landing with several doors. He opened them all and invited her to look around.

Three bedrooms, charmingly furnished, two bathrooms, and a small room which she could see would be very handy for a number of purposes—a sewing-room, somewhere to do the ironing or write letters, even put an unexpected guest or house a baby's cradle.

She joined him on the landing. 'It's all quite perfect. Just the kitchen needs something done to it.'

'Yes—come back downstairs; there's one more room to see.'

Just outside the kitchen door was another, opening on to a large, pleasant room, quite empty. 'I thought this might be turned into a bed-sitting-room for the caretaker...' He leaned his vast person against one wall and waited for Mary to speak.

'It's big enough to divide up. A shower-room at one end; no need for a kitchen but he'd need an electric kettle. A divan bed, chairs and a table, warm curtains and some sort of a fire. A nice russet-red, so that it looks welcoming.' She paused. 'That's only what I think,' she said apologetically. 'I dare say you have your own ideas.'

'I asked you to give me some advice, Mary. I'm grateful. I'll get the whole thing started as soon as possible.'

'Will you? But perhaps whoever comes here might not like it—the colours and so on.'

'I don't imagine that the caretaker will mind what colour his curtains are as long as the kitchen functions; he won't bother his head with colour schemes.'

She gave him a candid look. 'I wasn't thinking of the caretaker. Supposing you marry?'

'Ah, yes. Well, we can cross that bridge when we come to it.' He added slowly, 'Probably she will change her mind and I shall have it redecorated—that will be no problem.'

I must be mad, thought Mary, offering ideas about the place when it should be Ilsa doing so. Why didn't he bring her down here while she was staying with him?

'Did Ilsa come here?' The question popped out before she could stop it.

He seemed to find nothing strange in her question. 'No, not this time.' He closed the door and they went back into the kitchen. 'Shall we have our picnic? We could go into the garden.'

It wasn't just sandwiches; there were little rolls, butter in a covered dish, several cheeses, chicken drumsticks, miniature sausage rolls and a pork pie, as well as custards in little glasses, strawberries and clotted cream. There were china plates, cutlery, linen napkins and bottles of tonic water and lemonade. They sat on a wooden bench at the end of the garden, and even though it was still rather a dull day it was full of colour.

'You must have a very good gardener,' said Mary, her mouth full of chicken.

'He comes in each week, and I enjoy pottering around when I'm down here.'

He made no demur when she suggested that they might go back. 'If you don't mind,' she added, 'but Mother expects us for tea.'

Richard, happily tired after a day nosing around the garden, flopped on to the back seat and went to sleep, and Mary, nicely full, envied him. It would never do to fall asleep, though; she racked her brains for small talk and was affronted when Professor van Rakesma said, 'Don't bother to make conversation. Have a nap if you like.'

Which caused her to be wide awake on the instant. 'I am not in the least tired,' she told him frostily. All the same, she kept quiet, sensing that he was busy with his thoughts. It must be because I love him, she decided silently, that I can guess his moods. I do hope Ilsa loves him too.

She mustn't think about that. For lack of anything better, she began to recite silently 'The Lay of the Last Minstrel' which, while boring her, kept her mind off him.

Polly came running out as he drew up outside the house. 'Good, just in time; I've put the kettle on...'

He had got out to open Mary's door and free Richard. 'I must drive straight back, Polly. I am so sorry; I would have enjoyed having tea with you all, but I have an appointment and I'm going away very early in the morning.'

To Holland, thought Mary miserably, and said brightly, 'Then we mustn't keep you. Thank you for a lovely day; I enjoyed it.'

'I too, Mary. Please make my apologies to your parents.' He whistled to Richard, dropped a kiss on Polly's cheek, got into his car and drove away.

'Did you have a lovely day?' asked Polly.

'Quite perfect.' There would never be another day like it.

CHAPTER EIGHT

IT WAS on the following Saturday, shortly before Mr Bell closed his shop, that Professor van Rakesma came into it. Mary, parcelling up books for a peppery old retired colonel, faltered at the sight of him, so that the brown paper came loose and she had to begin all over again while the colonel muttered. Her heart was thumping so loudly that she felt sure that everyone there could hear it, and no amount of self-control could prevent the colour in her cheeks.

Professor van Rakesma, pausing in the doorway, studied her from under lowered lids, wishing that he could forget her and get on with his hitherto satisfactory life. But somehow she had disrupted it woefully. He bade her a cool good day and went in search of Mr Bell, collected the books put aside for him and went to the door where, much against his will, he turned round and went to the shelves that she was tidying before going home.

'I should like some more of your advice, Mary.'

He sounded faintly annoyed so she answered coolly, 'I'm going home in a few minutes, Professor van Rakesma. Perhaps another time?'

'Now, I'm afraid. A question of crockery for the kitchen at the cottage. I'm going there tomorrow and the decorator will be there. Would you come back with me to my flat now and tell me which to have? It won't delay you for more than an hour; you can phone your mother from my car.'

'He who hesitates...' Mary hesitated, and was lost. 'Very well, just as long as it doesn't take more than an hour.'

He nodded. 'I'll be outside.'

She had had no idea where he lived. The graceful house in Cheyne Walk enchanted her; she stood on the step before the door and looked over her shoulder at the river across the road; to live there would be very satisfying. The door opened and Fred, his face composed into no expression, held it wide.

'Ah, Fred. Miss Pagett has come to advise me on the china. It's in the kitchen? Mary, this is Fred, my manservant and right hand.'

Mary put out a hand and shook Fred's.

'A pleasure, miss,' he said, and meant it. Here was a fine-looking young lady, with lovely brown eyes and an enchanting smile, worth a hundred of that Mrs van Hoeven. Fred, a staunch Methodist, sent up a brief and urgent prayer on behalf of his master.

He led the way to the kitchen, so that this delightful lady could look around her, and offered her a chair. The crockery was spread all over the solid kitchen table. There were several samples of various patterns and colours and she studied them carefully.

'They are all pretty; I like that one there, the biscuit-coloured background with the yellow crocuses and the green handles.'

'Good,' said Professor van Rakesma. 'Fred, where did we put the patterns of materials?'

Fred opened a drawer. 'Here we are, miss.' Mary sat down again and fingered the samples. They were all lovely, but she made her choice finally and the professor said, 'While you are here what about the curtains for the bed-sitter?'

She chose those too, and then got up to go with a murmur about getting home.

'A cup of tea first; Fred, we'll be in the sitting-room.'

'Really——' began Mary.

'Yes, yes, I know. Tea will only take ten minutes, though, and you'll be home at the time you told your mother. Come in here.'

'Oh,' breathed Mary, rotating slowly in the middle of the room. 'How beautiful and—lived in, if you see what I mean. You must be very happy living here.'

'I'm glad you like it. Come and sit down. You're still enjoying your work at Mr Bell's shop?'

'Yes, very much—and he is so kind; I know so little about the book world, but I'm learning.'

Fred came in then with the tea-tray; silver teapot, china cups so thin that one could almost see through them, a plate of little cakes and another of tiny cucumber sandwiches. These he placed on a small table beside Mary. It was the best he could do at such short notice; if she came again he would make sure that he had one of his chocolate cakes ready for her...

She thanked him with a smile and the professor, watching, admired the way her tip-tilted nose wrinkled when she smiled. A charming nose, he conceded, and accepted a cup of tea while he talked easily about this and that. She answered him readily enough, but he sensed her reserve behind the pleasant manner and wondered why it was there. He had to admit that he found her interesting; he would like to know more about her...

He was secretly amused when she said briskly, 'Thank you for my tea. I must go home now.' He wasn't a conceited man, but he was well aware that he was sought after by the younger ladies of his acquaintance—not one of whom would have wished to leave him so promptly.

He said, 'Of course,' so readily that she wondered if she had stayed too long, and made no bones about going then and there.

Fred, on the look out, was there to open the door for them. He beamed his thanks at her appreciation of her tea and stood watching them drive away. Now that, he reflected, was the right kind of young lady for his master to wed—not that he had shown any special interest in her, more was the pity. He went back to the kitchen and phoned his Syl, who listened patiently and finally said, 'Well, we have to leave it to fate, don't we?'

'If fate needs a hand I'm more than willing,' said Fred.

Invited to come indoors with rather a lack of enthusiasm, Professor van Rakesma made himself agreeable to Mrs Pagett, allowed himself to be led away by Mr Pagett to look at some old document in Anglo-Saxon, spent ten minutes with Polly and Richard in the garden, declined coffee or a drink and then went back home, his goodbyes affable and, in Mary's case, cool.

'The girl is taking up too much of my time,' he told Richard. 'What is more, I find her unsettling.'

Mary finished getting the supper which Polly had started to cook. He was going to his cottage but he hadn't invited her to go again. There was no reason why he should. She knew quite well that she wasn't at her best in his company; her efforts to behave as though she considered him a mere acquaintance were inhibiting. All the same . . . perhaps Ilsa would be coming soon, to see the place for herself and approve the alterations. She wouldn't approve, of course, if she discovered that Mary had chosen the curtains and china.

'Well,' said Mary reasonably, 'neither would I!' Bingo, eating his supper, raised his head for a moment and stared at her; his feline ears had caught the unhappiness in her voice.

The professor didn't go alone; his new caretaker went with him. Nathaniel Potts had made a good recovery. He was a small man but wiry, with a round face and a fringe of grey hair. His eyes were blue and guileless and Fred, having met him, had pronounced him just the job. 'Nice old codger,' he'd observed. 'Just the thing for the cottage, sir. He'll settle in a treat.'

It was apparent immediately he followed Professor van Rakesma into the place that he was just right there. 'I can live here?' he wanted to know. 'Why, sir, it's beyond my wildest dreams.'

'Good. We'll go into your duties presently; I suggest that we go along to the pub and have a sandwich, then we can come back here and make sure that you have everything you need. I'll be down some time next weekend. Sometimes I come on the spur of the moment, so keep a stock of basic food in the fridge. See that you eat properly and look after yourself. The doctor here is a good man; I know him slightly. Go to him if you are worried. You have my phone number; Fred will always be able to get hold of me if I'm needed.'

The professor drove back to Cheyne Walk that evening. Nathaniel Potts had settled in quickly, a look on his face as though he had just won the pools. 'I can't

believe it,' he had said to him. 'I'd just about given up...
You won't regret it, sir...'

Mary had little opportunity to brood over her own
worries; her father had told her that he still owed the
bank money. 'I shall have to repay it from my capital,'
he explained, 'which leaves our circumstances still more
strained. I shall be unable to give you any money this
week, my dear, as what I have must pay the gas bill.'

'Don't worry, Father, I can manage the housekeeping—although there's not much over for paying any
bills. How is the book going?'

'Another month or so.' He looked anxious. 'Of course
it will need to be typed before I can take it to my publishers. An expense...' He sighed. 'There is talk of a
publishing date for Christmas.'

'Oh, good,' said Mary, and managed a smile.
Christmas was months away—Polly would need a winter
coat before then, and she wanted a new hockey stick for
her birthday. Perhaps Mr Bell would suggest that she
worked an extra day. She went away to do the ironing,
thinking of all the dreadful things she would do to the
man who had swindled her father. A waste of time, she
told herself, but it would be nice if there was someone
she could moan to—Professor van Rakesma, for
instance.

There were fewer customers in the bookshop that
week; it was high summer now, and people had gone on
holiday. It gave her the opportunity to do some much
needed sorting out and rearranging while Mr Bell shut
himself in his office and browsed happily. It also gave
her the opportunity to think about the professor. Her
imagination ran riot, picturing him in his fine flat, en-

tertaining friends, driving to their houses in his splendid car—and perhaps Ilsa was there too. She had said that she would be returning...

Professor van Rakesma was certainly driving his splendid car—to and from the hospital or to his consulting-rooms, or speeding up one or other of the motorways, lending his skill for the benefit of some patient. Certainly he had no leisure to entertain his friends or to visit them; it seemed to him that there was a positive epidemic of people with heart conditions requiring his aid, and his leisure was so sparse that when he did get a quiet hour or so all he wanted to do was to sit quietly at his desk and get on with his book.

Fred served him tempting meals, tut-tutting to himself when his employer didn't come home until all hours or left the flat at some unearthly time in the morning. A wife was what he needed, observed Fred to his Syl, but not that nasty woman who never said thank you and looked at him as though he ought not to have been there. 'In my own kitchen too,' said Fred.

By the end of another week things had quietened down a little; the professor had his meals at almost normal times and left the flat at a reasonable hour each morning. Life was back to normal again, allowing him time to think about Mary. It was some time since he had last seen her. He promised himself that on the following Saturday he would go along to Mr Bell's shop and see how she was getting on. They might go to the cottage on Sunday. Perhaps it would be a good idea to take Polly with them...

He didn't have to wait until Saturday, however.

* * *

Mary was tidying the kitchen after lunch on Monday when the phone rang and a voice announced that it was Polly's form mistress speaking and would Mary come and collect her sister, who had become ill.

'Have you sent for the doctor?' asked Mary. 'Is she sick or has she had an accident?'

'Very sick, feverish, and she doesn't seem at all herself. I suggest that you fetch her home and get her own doctor.'

Not a very satisfactory answer. Mary ran to give her mother a watered-down version of the lady's report and drove over to the school. Polly was lying down on a couch in the gym, her usually rosy cheeks waxen, her skin hot.

'Probably some sort of flu,' said the form mistress. 'I dare say a few days in bed will set her back on her feet.' She added, 'I'm sure she's looking better.'

Mary thought that she looked awful, but she didn't say so. 'I'll take her home and let you know what the doctor says.'

They helped Polly to the car between them and Mary, usually a cautious driver, was for once not cautious at all.

Getting Polly up to her room was no easy matter; she seemed half-conscious and unsteady on her feet and, once put to bed, lay there shivering despite her fever. Mary took her temperature and went to the phone.

Dr Hooper had just finished his morning rounds and was sitting down to a late lunch, but he promised to be there within the next fifteen minutes, which gave her time to go and tell her mother.

Mrs Pagett was devoted to her children, but the sight of any of them ill upset her badly. She went with Mary to see Polly and said in her wispy voice, 'Oh, Polly, darling, whatever is the matter?' She turned to Mary. 'She's had measles and chicken pox and mumps.'

'Yes, Mother. Dr Hooper will be here presently, and he will know what to do. Would you be a dear and get a tray of tea? I've interrupted his lunch and he might be glad of it.'

'Yes, yes, of course. You stay here, Mary; I'll let him in when he gets here.'

Doctor Hooper had known them all for a long time. He peered at Polly over his old-fashioned spectacles, took her pulse, looked at her tongue and took her temperature. Then he sat down on the bed.

'A nasty virus infection,' he said. 'There is a lot of it about. It hasn't got a name but it's very unpleasant. Antibiotics, I think, and stay in bed until you've finished the pills you'll be taking. Plenty to drink, and eat when you want to and whatever you fancy. You may be sick, but try and take no notice of that.'

He stood up. 'I'll leave you in Mary's capable hands.' He glanced at Mary's anxious face. 'Come downstairs with me, my dear, and I'll write that prescription and give you a few directions.'

Downstairs he warned, 'Even with the antibiotics Polly will probably get worse before she gets better. You can manage? You may have a few disturbed nights.'

He was right; Polly tossed and turned that night and most of the next day, peevishly refusing to eat or drink, wanting Mary to stay with her. Doctor Hooper came on the following day, said that he was satisfied that she was no worse, told Mary to get as much rest as she could and went away again. A busy GP, he still found time to

sit with Mrs Pagett for a few minutes and reassure her
that Polly would soon be better.

'You're sure? I can't settle to anything...'

Dr Hooper, who knew her well, said, 'My dear Mrs
Pagett, the best thing you can do is go to that little studio
of yours and return to your painting. She is in good
hands; Mary is a level-headed girl—a born nurse, if you
ask me. Can't think why she hasn't married before now.'

Although Polly was a little better on Thursday Mary
saw that it would be impossible to go to Mr Bell's. Very
reluctantly she phoned him, and was told by the kind
old man to stay at home until her sister was fit and well
again. 'I shall miss you,' said Mr Bell.

By some quirk of fate Professor van Rakesma, with half
an hour to spare that morning, decided that he had time
to call at Mr Bell's and collect a book he had wanted.
They passed the time of day briefly and he was on the
point of leaving when Mr Bell observed, 'I am missing
my helper at the moment...'

'Oh, why is that?' The professor had stopped on his
way out and turned round.

'Her sister—Polly, I believe her name is—is ill and
Mary must stay home and nurse her. A virus infection,
I understand. She is quite poorly.'

He was surprised at the look on his companion's face.
'Mary is a most efficient girl; I imagine she is managing
very well.'

'Yes, yes, I'm sure she is. Let us hope she will be back
soon.'

An hour later, between appointments, the professor
left his consulting-rooms and sought out his receptionist, who was elderly and devoted and never at a loss.

'Mrs Rigley——' she had always been and would always be Mrs Rigley, although they were the best of friends '—I need to speak to a doctor somewhere in Hampstead. Probably on the Golders Green side. The name of the patient I want to ask about is a Polly Pagett.' He smiled. 'Am I asking the impossible?'

'Give me a little time,' Mrs Rigley told him calmly. 'It is by no means impossible, but probably a lengthy business.'

It was five o'clock and he was on the point of leaving the hospital when she telephoned him. 'Doctor Hooper, Professor; I have his address and phone number here.'

'Mrs Rigley, you're an angel.' He made a note of them. 'Has it hindered you too much? Don't stay late...'

'No, Professor. You have only one patient here tomorrow morning, at noon. You are to lunch at the hospital before the meeting there.' She added briskly, 'I've booked Mrs Morley for six o'clock tomorrow evening. She can't get here any sooner.'

'Thank you.' He wished her goodbye and rang off and dialed Dr Hooper's number.

Half an hour later he let himself into his flat, and as usual Fred came into the hall to meet him.

'I must go out again Fred; can you hold dinner back for a while?'

'No problem, sir!'

'While I'm gone go through the food in the house and see if there's anything suitable for a young girl who feels pretty rough. I'll take it with me in the morning. I'll need to leave here around half-past seven.'

'I'll see to it, sir.' Fred, dying of curiosity, kept his face expressionless and the professor took pity on him. 'The young sister of Miss Pagett has been taken ill; I've spoken to her doctor, who has no objection to my paying a call on her. I'll take Richard with me.'

He stopped on the way to buy flowers. For Polly, of course.

Mary opened the door in answer to his knock. She was tired, and her hair had escaped from its usual neat French pleat, her nose needed powdering and she longed to put her feet up. She stood and stared at him.

'Oh, I'm so glad...' she said, and caught her tongue between her teeth just in time. 'Polly's ill.' For a moment she thought she might burst into tears. She swallowed them back and added, 'You know?'

'Mr Bell told me. Dr Hooper has no objection to my seeing her if you would like that.'

'Oh, I would—and so would she. Do come in. Do you know Dr Hooper?'

'Er—no, a telephone acquaintance, shall we say? You need a night's sleep, Mary.'

'I'm quite all right. Polly gets restless during the night——'

'You sit with her?'

'Until she settles down again. Would you like to come upstairs? Mother is painting and Father is not back yet.'

'There is no one to relieve you?'

'There's no need. Mother gets upset if any of us is ill, but she sits with Polly...'

She opened Polly's door and he followed her in. Polly was lying staring at the ceiling but she turned her head as they went in. 'Professor van Rakesma—how did you know that I was ill? Mary, did you tell him?'

He had come to stand by the bed and picked up one of her hands. 'No, Mary didn't tell me. You feel quite wretched, don't you? But a few more days in bed and you'll begin to feel your old self again. Dr Hooper gave me a good report of you.'

He sat himself down on the side of the bed. 'These are to make you feel better,' he said, and laid the flowers on the quilt.

'Thank you, they're lovely. Are you going to stay for a little while?'

He turned to look at Mary. 'Half an hour, if I may? While you do whatever you want to downstairs.'

He wasn't only the man she loved but he was kind and thoughtful too, and someone to lean on, albeit metaphorically. She nipped smartly back to the kitchen, saw to the supper, fed Bingo and went to tell her mother that they had a visitor.

'Bless the man,' said Mrs Pagett. 'Just when he's most needed. Is he staying to supper?'

'No, he has to go very shortly; he's sitting with Polly while I get the supper.'

Mrs Pagett looked conscience-stricken. 'Oh, dear, I could have done that—or sat with Polly; I did mean to...'

Mary bent to kiss her parent. 'Darling, don't worry! There's almost nothing to do. Can you spare a moment to see Professor van Rakesma?'

'Yes, of course; I'll come now. Is your father back yet?'

'No. He should be here at any minute, though.'

They went into the house together—Mary to the kitchen, Mrs Pagett to her younger daughter's bedroom. Mary heard her come downstairs presently with the professor. They both came into the kitchen and she paused in puréeing the potatoes to ask what he thought of Polly.

'Doubtless a virulent virus—luckily Polly is very fit and healthy. She should begin to feel better within another forty-eight hours. She will be off-colour for a week or two, though.'

He declined her offer of coffee, bade her a friendly goodnight and went out to his car with Mrs Pagett, who then wandered back into the kitchen. 'Such an agreeable man. I wonder how he found out which doctor we have?' She added vaguely, 'Well, I suppose they all know each other.'

Polly had brightened up considerably at his visit, but her sleep that night was fitful. She was too hot, too cold, thirsty, her legs ached . . .

Mary gave up her bed presently, and sat in a chair near her in her nightie and dressing-gown; she dozed fitfully too. Some time after six o'clock she slept deeply, and was roused by the doorbell. Polly still slept, and the house was quiet, but a glance at the clock told her that it was half-past eight. She flew downstairs and unbolted the door; it would be Mrs Blackett, she thought, forgetting it was Friday . . .

The professor, with Richard beside him, and bearing a large hamper, stood in the porch. Mary stood gaping at him, still not quite awake, then she said in a wobbly voice, 'I overslept,' and burst into tears.

Professor van Rakesma, never a man to hesitate, bore her gently back into the hall, closed the door behind the three of them, put the hamper on the nearest chair and took her in his arms. He didn't speak until her sobs dwindled into sniffs and watery gasps. 'Another bad night? This won't do, you know. We'll have you lying in bed beside Polly . . .'

He mopped her face and thought how beautiful she was—hair in a glorious tangle, a pink nose and puffy eyes, and swathed in a shapeless dressing-gown only fit for the dustbin. The thought struck him with some force that he had fallen in love at last—that, indeed, he had been in love for some time. But first things first.

'Come into the kitchen and put the kettle on and I'll unpack this. Bingo won't object to Richard?'

'No, he's the mildest of cats.' Mary gave a great sniff. 'I'm sorry to be such a fool.'

'Think nothing of it. Are your mother and father still in their room?'

'Yes. I usually take them a cup of tea about eight o'clock.'

'Shall we have a cup first? I'll get breakfast while you dress.'

'Get breakfast? But can you cook?'

'Of course I can cook. A limited menu, mind, but would scrambled eggs do?'

'Oh,' said Mary. 'I'm so glad you're here.'

She was suddenly shy, and put a hand up to her tousled hair. 'Oh, dear, I'm sorry to be so—so——'

He didn't let her finish. 'Shall we have that cup of tea?'

'Yes—yes, of course.'

He put the hamper on the kitchen table and started to unpack it while the kettle boiled: a cold roasted chicken, an egg custard in a pretty little dish, tiny fairy-like cakes, a bottle of champagne, a milk jelly in a delicate shade of pink, a box of brown eggs, and a nicely arranged pile of small crisp biscuits on a patterned plate.

Mary, coming to look, said, 'My goodness, how tempting it all looks. Polly will love everything.'

'Fred did his best. He's a good cook!'

'He made all these? But how kind—and kinder still of you to have thought of it.'

He said quietly, 'I like Polly.'

They drank their tea quickly and Mary carried a tray up to her parents, went to peep at Polly and then to dress. She groaned aloud when she caught sight of herself in the looking-glass. What must he have thought? she wondered.

The professor kept his thoughts to himself and concentrated on getting breakfast. He laid the table, broke the eggs, cut bread and set to work on arranging a tray for Polly. He had finished when Mary came downstairs again, this time very neat and tidy, not a hair out of place, although she hadn't had time to do her face. Looking at her, he decided that she looked even better in her old dressing-gown, especially with her hair all over the place.

Mr and Mrs Pagett came down next, greeting the professor as though it were quite normal to come down to breakfast and find him there. 'I looked in on Polly,' said Mrs Pagett. 'She's still asleep. How delicious these eggs are, Mary.'

'Professor van Rakesma got breakfast, Mother.'

Mrs Pagett took this in her stride. 'Then you are to be congratulated, Professor.' She caught sight of the delicacies set out on the dresser. 'And just look at these— for Polly? How very kind. She *is* getting better?'

His answer was quietly reassuring. They had reached the toast and marmalade when Polly's voice, rather querulous, reached them.

'May I go up and see her?' asked the professor. 'Perhaps another face...'

He sat down on the bed and smiled at Polly's rather white face. She put out a sweaty hand and took his. 'I did hope you'd come,' she told him. 'And you did. How did you know?'

'I have spies everywhere.' He took her pulse and noted that it was slower; she looked less feverish too. 'You're on the turn,' he observed. 'Dr Hooper is going to be pleased with you. Now, to oblige both your doctors, you must start to eat a little. I brought some food with me—Fred, my manservant, got up early and filled a hamper, so don't hurt his feelings by not eating everything in it.'

'I'll try, I promise you, and do please thank him. Does he look after you? Is that the man Ilsa wanted to sack? She said he wasn't suitable...'

'I find him entirely suitable, and I hope he will stay with me until we are both very old men. He's going to be married at Christmas to a rather nice girl called Syl.'

'Will she work for you too?'

'Oh, yes; we shall need extra help.'

'Are you going to get married?' Polly had heaved herself up against her pillows and he leaned forward and shook them up.

'Yes.'

'Not to Ilsa?'

'No.' He smiled slowly as she stared up at him.

'Who to?' She smiled too, a wide grin of expectancy. 'Tell me.'

He told her and she leaned forward and flung her arms round his neck. 'It's a secret between us,' he pointed out.

'Of course. I'll not breathe a word. You're sure?' She glanced at his face. 'Yes, you are! That was a silly

question. Do you suppose you would mind if I called
you Roel?'

'I should be delighted; I am quite weary of being addressed as Professor van Rakesma; it makes me feel ex-
cessively middle-aged.' He stood up. 'I must go. I'll come
and see you again, but not tomorrow—the day after. I
shall expect to see you plump and rosy-cheeked and at
least sitting in a chair.'

He went presently, taking Mr Pagett, who wanted to
go to the British Museum Library, with him, and Mrs
Pagett, after helping Mary clear away the breakfast and
putting everything away in the wrong places, drifted
down to the shed.

Mary whisked upstairs, washed Polly's face and hands,
brushed her hair and straightened her bed. 'Breakfast,'
she said. 'You should see what Professor van Rakesma
has brought for you. There are some dear little savoury
biscuits that his man Fred made specially for you and a
box of brown eggs. I'm going to scramble one for you
with some of those biscuits and you're going to eat the
lot.'

Rather to her surprise Polly said quite cheerfully that
she would.

Dr Hooper, when he came, pronounced her better.
'Another day in bed and then she may get up for a while.
I don't need to come for a day or two, but if you are
worried you know where I am.'

So when Professor van Rakesma came again two days
later, just as Mary was putting the kettle on for tea, he
found Polly sitting at the kitchen table, gobbling a milk
jelly and the last of the little cakes. This time he had
brought sponge fingers, a pot of salmon pâté and some
more of the little savoury biscuits, and it seemed quite

natural that he should sit down too and have his tea with her and Mary. Mrs Pagett was in her shed and Mary took her tea down to her.

'He's here again? Oh, good. I'll be up presently; I must just paint in these cherubs' faces.'

She joined them, ate several sponge fingers and expressed her relief that Polly had recovered.

'Ah, yes, Mrs Pagett. I was wondering if you would allow Polly to spend a few days at a cottage I have in Gloucestershire? There is a caretaker there and I'm sure you'd agree to Mary's going with her. It would be just the thing to set her on her feet again. It's very quiet but I'm sure they would find enough to do together.'

'You wouldn't be there?'

'No. I would, of course, drive them both down and bring them back.'

Polly's eyes were shining. 'Oh, may I, Mother, please . . .?'

Mary said nothing at all, but her heart galloped along at a great pace at the mere thought of it. Her mother might say no; she schooled her features into serenity.

'That would be good for Polly, wouldn't it? I thank you, Professor, most sincerely. I'm sure it will do her good, and we can manage for a few days without Mary; I'm quite sure she needs a rest too. Their father won't object, I know. When do you want them to go?'

'Saturday afternoon? And if you can manage for a week I could bring them back on the following Saturday morning.'

'Of course. Mary will fill the freezer with meals so that all I have to do is warm them up, won't you, dear? And Mrs Blackett will clean the house as usual.'

'That's settled, then.' He glanced at Mary. 'May Richard stay with you? He loves the cottage and Nathaniel will look after him.'

He went presently and Mary wandered upstairs in a delightful dream, to peer in cupboards and drawers and decide what to take with them.

She rang Mr Bell that evening; Polly was well enough to leave alone now, and she needed the money. He was delighted to have her back, even when she explained that she would be away again the following week. She heaved a sigh of relief and sat down to think out suitable meals for her mother while she was away.

She enjoyed being back at Mr Bell's; she was still tired from worry and lack of sleep but she had a week of doing nothing much to look forward to. She put every-thing ready before she left home on Saturday morning and, since Mr Bell allowed her to go home at three o'clock and the professor had said that he would come for her then, she allowed herself to feel the excitement which had been bubbling up inside her. The face she showed him as she got into the car was serene enough, however.

Polly, still pale, but excited, was waiting for them and, waved on their way by their parents, they got into the car with an equally excited Richard and a calm pro-fessor who drove away.

There was no need for Mary to talk on the journey; Polly hardly paused for breath, and when they reached the cottage and got out she stood staring at it. 'I don't believe it,' she cried. 'It's just like a dream, Roel; how can you bear to leave it?'

CHAPTER NINE

THE cottage looked at its best—Nathaniel had seen to it. The furniture glowed, there were flowers in all the rooms and the evening sun cast a soft light over everything; Mary paused in the hall and shook his hand and looked around her. 'It's quite perfect,' she said, and he beamed at her.

'I'm happy that you think so, miss.' He looked at the professor then, and was rewarded with an approving nod. 'The bedrooms are ready, sir, and there's supper laid in the dining-room.'

'Good, you've done excellently, Nathaniel. We'll bring in the cases and have supper at once for I must get back to town.' The professor looked at Mary. 'Would you go upstairs through that small door in the dining-room? Your rooms are at the front. We'll bring up your bags.'

Their rooms were charming, with sloping ceilings and sprigged wallpaper and satinwood beds and dressing-tables. There was a bathroom between them and Polly ran from one to the other, for once speechless with delight.

The men came up with their luggage and the professor said, 'Nathaniel will take you round the place later; I'm afraid I haven't the time; I'll have to go when we've had supper.'

Nathaniel, it seemed, could cook; there was a steak and kidney pie with a light-as-air crust, new potatoes and puréed spinach and after that he served up straw-

167

berries and clotted cream with macaroon biscuits. Since
the professor was undoubtedly anxious to be off they
didn't linger over the meal.

'Use the phone whenever you want to,' he told them.
'If you run short of money Nathaniel will let you have
whatever you need. I'll be down next Saturday morning.
Enjoy yourselves, and please take care of Richard for
me.'

They went out to the car with him and he bent to kiss
Polly's cheek. 'I shall expect to see you looking your
usual self,' he told her. He didn't say anything to Mary
but kissed her—a gentle, unhurried kiss which left her
pink and breathless.

It was easy to slip into the peace of their days. They slept
soundly, despite Mary's certainty that she would lie
awake every night and think about Professor van
Rakesma. His kiss had meant something—something he
hadn't been able to put into words in front of Polly and
Nathaniel. However, she told herself that she might be
thinking it meant more than he had intended.

Strangely, the thought didn't worry her; she slept
soundly every night and got up to eat a splendid breakfast
and walk to the village with Polly and a happy little dog
to do the shopping for Nathaniel. Her other offers of
help he gently refused.

'It's a real pleasure to have you young ladies here,
miss, and I've time enough to see to everything. The
professor has been down once or twice to see about the
alterations you suggested. Very satisfactory they are too;
the kitchen's a fair treat to work in—and if you would
care to see my bed-sitting-room?'

It had been furnished exactly as she had suggested too, and was as cosy as she had envisaged. 'You're happy here.' It was a statement not a question.

'Indeed I am, miss. I don't suppose the professor told you about me? I was down and out, you see; they found me in the park and brought me to St Justin's and he examined me. A heart attack, it was. He saved my life and then bless me if he doesn't offer me this job.' His nice, elderly face was very earnest. 'Cut my right hand off for him, I would.'

'I know,' said Mary. 'I know exactly how you feel.' They smiled at each other before she said briskly, 'Shall we go to the village and get those chops for you? He's a splendid butcher, isn't he?'

Polly was in her element; she had made friends in the village almost at once, besides which there was Richard to take for walks and the lovely garden in which to sit and do nothing. Every now and then she would say, 'I wonder what Roel's doing now?' Mary never answered, although she wondered too.

He was making careful plans which involved a good deal of telephoning on Mrs Rigley's part and several sessions with his senior registrar, as well as a number of phone calls to his home in Holland. It also meant a visit to Mr and Mrs Pagett...

The week was too quickly over; one day had slipped into the next and each one had been more delightful than the last. All the same, Mary longed for the weekend and Professor van Rakesma's arrival. 'And for heaven's sake call him Roel,' begged Polly, her own exuberant self once more. 'I do.'

He came on Saturday morning just as Nathaniel was getting the coffee. It was a lovely morning and he came straight through the house and out into the garden to find them sitting on the wooden bench at the far end.

Richard saw him first and rushed round in circles, barking his pleasure, while Polly raced across the lawn to fling herself at him.

'I'm well again—see? I'm getting fat; Nathaniel's such a marvellous cook. Mary's getting fat too!'

He dropped a kiss on her cheek and stared across her head at Mary, on her feet now and coming towards them. 'Not fat,' he said, 'just nicely curved in all the right places.'

The remark made her blush. All the same, she said, 'Hello, you're just in time for coffee. Would you like it out here? I'll go and tell Nathaniel...'

'I'll go,' said Polly, leaving Mary staring at him. After a moment she said, 'We've had a lovely week; Polly's quite well again and I feel fit enough to spring-clean the house and dust every one of Mr Bell's books.'

'Good. I've been talking to your parents; another week off won't hurt, Polly—but not here. I'm going over to Holland on Monday—will you both come with me?'

When she opened her mouth to speak he said, 'No, don't say anything until I've finished. Pleane is longing to see you both again and my mother will be delighted to meet you.'

He had spoken in a matter-of-fact way and she did her best to answer him in the same vein. 'It sounds very tempting, and how kind of you to think of it, but we haven't got passports...'

'Visitors'—obtainable at any post office.'

'Yes, well—but I've been away from home for a week; I really ought to stay—and—and...'

'Do the washing and the dusting and cook the meals? I know. Will you leave that side of it to me? Maisie— remember her?— would love to spend a week with your parents; she likes a change from nursing now and then.'

'But she is NHS. They'd never allow her to come.'

'NHS? I don't remember saying that she worked for the NHS. She works for me and several other consultants who may need a private nurse from time to time.'

She thought about that. 'Were you paying her, then? When she came to Great Aunt Thirza's house? Because if you were I owe you money for her fees.'

'By all means pay me back, but later. We're discussing a brief trip to Holland at the moment. Will you come?' And as she hesitated and Polly came dancing out he said, 'Polly, would you like to come to Holland with me? Just to round off your convalescence?'

'Me? And Mary? Roel, you darling, of course I would. When are we going?'

'You can't disappoint Polly,' said the professor unfairly.

'Well, if you think she needs a little more time before she goes back to school... You're sure your mother won't mind? I mean, she doesn't know anything about us.'

'I imagine Pleane has told her a very great deal.'

'Where do you live?' she asked, aware that she stood no chance against the two of them, and not much caring.

'In the north—Friesland. A small village near Leeuwarden.' He didn't offer more than that and she didn't like to ask.

'Mary, say you'll come,' said Polly. 'You must, just think—just lovely to see another country; Mary, you must, you must!'

The Professor added quietly, 'Yes, Mary, you must.'

She nodded slowly. 'Very well, it would be most—most interesting. Just for a few days.'

'A week.'

'Will you be there?' She couldn't resist asking that, not seeing the gleam in his eyes.

'Yes, most of the time. I shall have to go to Leeuwarden, and down to Amsterdam and The Hague, but I shall have some time to show you something of Friesland.' He added, 'Besides, Pleane will be there.'

They drank their coffee then, and presently Polly took him away to look for water voles living by the little stream which bordered the end of the garden, and Richard went with them, leaving Mary alone with her thoughts.

She was mad to agree to go, she knew that; she would probably meet Ilsa, who would demonstrate the fact of her impending marriage to him in no uncertain way. She would put up with that just for the delight of being with him for a little longer. I'll come back home, she reflected, and go back to Mr Bell and make myself indispensable to him. And in a few months, when Father's book is published and everything's all right again, I'll take the librarian's exams and make a career for myself.

Even as she thought about it she knew that it was highly unlikely; there would never be enough money to make it possible. She choked back self-pity and went to find Nathaniel. They had become firm friends during the past week and she wanted to be sure that he would look after himself properly when there was no one at the cottage.

They drove back to Hampstead after lunch. Nathaniel had given her a bunch of flowers from the garden and wrung her hand. 'I hope I'll see you again, miss, that I do—and the young lady too. It's been a pleasure looking after you.'

She thanked him, told him to take care of himself, and got into the car beside the professor, and, with Polly chattering away from the back of the car and Richard expressing his pleasure at being with his master again, they drove back through the fading summer countryside.

'It must be beautiful here in the autumn,' said Mary, making conversation.

'Yes, indeed.' He wickedly allowed her to wring the subject of the autumn—indeed, of all the seasons—dry.

'Can you be ready by Monday, early afternoon?'

'I expect so, if I start as soon as we get home.' She sounded a bit tart. 'It isn't very long. And I must phone Mr Bell...'

'Ah—well, I was there during the week and mentioned that you might be going with me; he thought it a splendid idea.'

'Did he? Did he really?' She hoped that she wouldn't get the sack after so much time away from the shop. It was as well for her peace of mind that she didn't know that Mr Bell had already engaged a suitable applicant in her place. 'For,' Professor van Rakesma had told him, 'I intend to marry Mary.'

Mr Bell, a romantic at heart, had been delighted.

Her mother and father were delighted too to see her back, but enthusiastic about their trip to Holland. 'Maisie came to see us today,' said her mother. 'Such a very nice person; she will do the housekeeping while

you're away, dear, so we shall be quite comfortable.' She
turned to Roel. 'You'll stay for tea, Roel?'

He shook his head. 'There are some patients I must
see this evening. I'll be here on Monday afternoon—
we'll catch the night ferry from Harwich.'

Presently he took his leave and Mary, who hadn't forgotten his kiss, received his casual nod with a cool one
of her own. He hadn't meant it, she thought bitterly.
Then, since she was a fair-minded girl, she thought, why
should he? He was going to marry Ilsa. He had probably
been amusing himself. She didn't quite believe
that, though.

The weekend was a frenzy of activity; the washing machine laboured non-stop, Mary ironed and pressed and
packed once again, and put the house to rights after Mrs
Blackett's half-hearted onslaughts with the furniture
polish. She made neat lists for Maisie's guidance too,
and on Monday morning hurried to the shops with the
last of the housekeeping money to buy groceries.

She had forgotten that she would need money in
Holland so it was an agreeable surprise when her father
called her into his study. 'You'll need pocket money,' he
told her. 'My publishers have advanced me something
on royalties; take this, my dear, and don't worry. I have
sufficient to keep us going nicely for some time.'

'Father, how splendid. I'm so glad. You won't need
to give Maisie much; I've stocked up with quite a lot of
food. You're sure that you and Mother will be all right?'

'Quite sure, my dear. You've earned this holiday; enjoy
yourself.'

The professor arrived punctually, this time without
Richard, and this time Mary said firmly that she would

sit in the back. He made no demur, and as they drove to Harwich he and Polly chatted almost without pause. Mary, replying to the odd remark thrown at her from over a shoulder, told herself that she didn't mind.

She wasn't sophisticated enough to ignore the delights of the ferry. She and Polly shared a cabin which they considered the acme of comfort, and then joined the professor at dinner. Neither of them had any fears about seasickness; they enjoyed every morsel put before them, drank the glass of wine he chose for them and went to their beds, to sleep soundly until the stewardess wakened them early the next morning with tea and toast.

They were among the first away, and the Rolls, once on the motorway, travelled fast. They were approaching Delft when he suggested coffee and parked the car in the great square in the centre of the lovely little town, and took them to a small café overlooking it. As well as coffee, he ordered *krentenbollen*, a rich version of the currant bun, and they sat for a while, eating them and watching the cars going to and fro, while he told them of the Nieuwe Kerk, towering over one end of the market square.

They drove on presently, going north, bypassing Leiden and then Amsterdam, making for the *Afsluitdijk* motorway which would bring them to Friesland.

The countryside was different here, with wide open fields separated from each other by narrow, water-filled ditches; the farms, with their great barns built on to them at the back, looked prosperous, and there were cows everywhere. Every now and then there was a glimpse of water too.

'The lakes,' said the professor. 'We live beside one.'

He turned away from the main road presently, along a narrow brick road, which led away into the distance to a cluster of trees. When they were reached they were found to surround a village built beside a large stretch of water.

'Is this your home?' asked Polly.

'Yes, just a little further.' He drove through the village street, lined with small houses with shining windows and spotless white curtains, and, when the road rounded a bend, drove between stone pillars, along a short drive and stopped before a gabled house. Its flat front was pierced by several rows of large windows, the front door was massive and solid, and there was a wrought-iron balcony above it.

Mary's heart sank; it was all so grand. They hadn't got the right clothes for a start; his mother wouldn't approve of them...

The front door was flung open and Pleane came running out to fling her arms around her brother's neck. 'Roel, you're here at last. Polly, come on—come with me. Mary, it's lovely to see you.'

She went ahead with Polly, and Roel turned to Mary. 'This is my home, Mary,' he told her. 'Welcome to it.'

After that everything was all right. True, his mother at first glance looked rather formidable, for she was tall and stout and her blue eyes had the same direct look as her son's, but her welcome was warm; they were led away to tidy themselves, up a grand curving staircase, along a wide landing and into two rooms overlooking the grounds at the back of the house.

Left alone, Polly came dancing into Mary's room. 'Isn't this just too gorgeous for words? He never said, did he? Perhaps he's so used to it that he doesn't notice how grand it is. He's going to be here all day tomorrow as well as today; he said he'd show us everything.'

Mary, making sure that her hair was securely pinned, observed, 'It's certainly very beautiful; he must miss it.'

'Yes, but when he marries he'll come here more often; he said so.' She went to peer at herself in the triple mirror. 'His mother doesn't live here, you know. There's a house in Leeuwarden.'

'How do you know all this?'

'I asked, of course. We're friends, Roel and me.'

'I,' said Mary. 'We'd better go down.'

The house might have been grand but the atmosphere was homely. In the vast drawing-room, where they had drinks before lunch, there was knitting on a chair, books and magazines scattered on a side-table, a tabby cat perched on the window-seat and two dogs lolling by the open French window.

They were big shaggy beasts, with little yellow eyes and a great many teeth. 'Bouviers,' said the professor. 'William and Mary; they look fierce but they're your friends for life once you belong.'

Mary put out a balled fist, and had it sniffed and then gently licked. 'They're splendid creatures. I don't suppose Richard has ever seen them?'

'No, I'm not sure if they would like each other.'

Any doubts Mary had had about their welcome were dispelled by the time lunch was over. His mother might have looked severe but her smile was gentle and kind and she laughed a lot. 'Come and sit by me and tell me about yourself,' she invited Mary as they drank their coffee. 'Pleane is going to show Polly the garden and Roel has some business to attend to.'

A pleasant hour passed while Mevrouw van Rakesma chatted and asked questions in the nicest possible manner, and since there was no sense in not being honest Mary answered truthfully.

'What do you intend to do with your future, my dear?' asked her hostess kindly.

Mary told her. 'If I can pass the exams I can make quite a career out of it. Not necessarily in a library—museums and large country houses sometimes have good jobs going.'

'You don't wish to marry?'

'I'd like to marry, but I'm not going to,' Mary said calmly.

They had a splendid day after that—touring the house, listening to its history, hearing about the village and the people who lived in it.

The next morning they walked there with the professor, who seemed to know everyone who lived there by name. They went into the little whitewashed church and looked at the names of long-dead van Rakesmas, carved into its stone floor, and they walked by the lake, watching the yachts, of which there were any number.

'People come for the weekend and their holidays—it's possible to sail from one lake to another.'

'Have you got a yacht?' Polly wanted to know.

'Yes. Perhaps I'll have the time to take you out on it.'

'But not tomorrow?'

'Tomorrow I have to work, and the next day, but I'll only be away for two days.'

He had gone by the time they got down for breakfast the next day and that morning Ilsa came.

Polly and Pleane had taken the dogs for a walk down by the lake and Mary was sitting with Mevrouw van Rakesma when Ton, who looked after the house with his wife, opened the door to announce that Mevrouw van Hoeven had called.

He was pushed aside by Ilsa, and Mevrouw van Rakesma frowned. Her greeting was pleasant enough, though. 'This is unexpected, Ilsa; I thought you were in The Hague.'

'I met the director of the Leeuwarden Children's Hospital yesterday; he told me that Roel was in Holland.' She turned to Mary. 'What are you doing here?'

Mary said, 'Hello, Ilsa. We're paying a visit. We came over with Roel.'

Ilsa's eyes narrowed. 'Really?' She turned back to Mevrouw van Rakesma. 'I wanted to see Roel; he's here of course?'

'He's away—will be for a few days. Do sit down; Ton will bring coffee.'

'Where is he? I've got the car...'

'He didn't say; I know he's visiting several hospitals and will be away for several days. Would you like to leave a message, Ilsa? He'll be sorry he's missed you.'

Ilsa had recovered her charm. 'No—no message. I'm quite sure he'll ring me as soon as he is free. After all, it's to see me that he has come.' She glanced at Mary as she spoke. 'We have a number of decisions to make.'

Her hostess said nothing to that and Ilsa went on, 'We saw so little of each other when Pleane and I were staying with him. I believe I must go back with him, so that we can get everything settled.'

'That would perhaps be best. Ah, here is the coffee.'

Ilsa was wearing gloves with her elegant outfit, so un-
suitable for her surroundings. She slipped them off, but
neither of her companions saw the ring on her engagement finger. She put the glove back on again, drank
her coffee, talking amusingly while she did so, and then
declared that she must go. 'I'm lunching in Dokkum,'
she explained. 'Such a dull little town, I always think.'

She made her graceful goodbyes to Mevrouw van
Rakesma and turned to Mary. 'Do walk to the car with
me and tell me what you think of Friesland—so different from Hampstead, is it not? And this is such a
pleasant house.' She was leading the way out of the lofty
wide hall. 'I have always loved it; it will be delightful to
live here.'

They reached the car but she made no attempt to get
into it. 'I must say I admire you for trying, Mary. Did
you really think that you stood a chance against me?
Roel and I have had an understanding for years, and we
shall marry shortly.'

'There was no reason why he should tell me, Ilsa,'
Mary said quietly.

'Oh, yes, there was. You may think you're concealing
your feelings very well, my dear, but he saw through you
weeks ago. He's too kind to say anything to you, but
surely you have the wit to see that he brought you here
so that you would understand once and for all that he
is merely a friend, helping someone who needs a job and
money; he's always helping people... You don't have
to believe me, but I'm going to see him now, for I know
where he is.'

'I don't believe you,' said Mary in a proud little voice.
When Ilsa took off her glove once more and held out

her hand, and she saw the diamond sparkling there, though, she knew.

'We shall announce our engagement and marry very shortly.' She smiled at Mary. 'But of course you won't be at the wedding.'

She got into the car, waved gaily and drove away. Mary watched her go; she had thought during the last few days that Roel was growing fond of her, and she couldn't forget his kiss but, despite disliking Ilsa, she could see that she might be speaking the truth. She had spoken with such certainty. It all made sense too. Roel had never mentioned his future plans, but then why should he since he knew that she wasn't included in them? His kindness had been just that and nothing more.

She was walking slowly back to the house when Pleane and Polly joined her. 'Did we see Ilsa driving through the village? Did she come here?' Pleane wanted to know. 'She hasn't been near us for ages, not since we came back from London.'

'She called to see your mother; she's on her way to have lunch in Dokkum.'

'I bet she was surprised to see you,' said Polly.

'Well, yes, I think she was.'

'Was she friendly? What did she talk about?'

'Oh, nothing much. Did you have a good walk?'

She's upset, thought Polly, and began a long description of where they had been, and when they joined Mevrouw van Rakesma she was careful not to mention Ilsa, although Pleane said something softly in Dutch to her mother.

A good cry, that's what I want, thought Mary, joining in the talk, smiling and nodding and not taking in a word. If only they hadn't come; if only they had stayed at home

and got on with a life which had nothing to do with
Roel. There was no help for it, though; they would have
to stay until he drove them home again and she could
concentrate on forgetting him. Polly must forget him too,
and she would be hurt, for the pair of them had become
firm friends.

He was coming home in the evening—in time for
dinner, he had said; Mary got into her one festive dress
and took a good look at herself in the pier glass. It was
a sober garment, meant to last several years—dateless
and simple and mousy brown. Not a colour she would
have chosen from choice, but it had been cheap in the
sales and was the kind of dress which would pass muster
almost anywhere. If she hadn't been so pretty it would
have been a disaster; as it was it did nothing for her.
Not that it matters, she told herself.

They sat in the drawing-room waiting for him; the
dinner hour passed, and his mother had just wondered
out loud what had happened to him when Ton came to
tell her that the professor had phoned to say that he
would be unable to return home until the next day and
expressed his regrets.

'An unexpected meeting,' said Mevrouw van Rakesma,
translating for Mary and Polly's benefit. 'We will dine
at once, Ton,' she said, and then in English, 'One can
never be sure of anything with a doctor in the family,
can one?'

They played Monopoly and Trivial Pursuit after dinner
until bedtime, and Mary was thankful when her hostess
declared that she was going to bed.

'Let William and Mary into the garden before you
come up,' she told Pleane. 'Mary, you look tired...'

So Mary went to her room too, undressed slowly and lay in the bath for a long time, making unlikely plans for her future which involved a great deal of hard work ending in success and a splendid career. She didn't believe any of it but it prevented her from crying. Only when she was in bed she gave up her ideas of being a career girl and thought about Roel, and cried into her pillow very quietly, so that Polly wouldn't hear.

Roel was there when they went down to breakfast, out in the garden with the dogs, and she was glad that there was time only to wish him good morning before his mother and Pleane joined them.

'A successful trip?' asked his mother, pouring the coffee.

'Yes. I must come over again in a couple of months— there's a seminar—and I may have to go to Brussels later on.'

'But you'll be at Cheyne Walk for the rest of the time?'

'Yes, although I intend to take a few weeks' holiday fairly soon.'

He caught Polly's eye and smiled a little. 'What have you been doing with yourselves?'

'Being lazy,' said Polly.

Pleane added, 'Ilsa came yesterday.'

'Yes.' He looked at Mary, who had her eyes on her plate. 'I know.'

So Ilsa had been truthful after all—that was why he hadn't come home. Mary crumbled toast and composed her face to a state of cheerfulness; to anyone not knowing her well it looked genuine, but Polly and Roel, knowing her well each in their own way, knew better.

'I'll take the dogs for a walk,' said Roel as they finished breakfast. 'Mary, a walk would do you good; come
with me.'

It was hard to think up an excuse in front of everyone
else there and she hesitated too long. 'You won't need
a jacket——' he glanced at her feet in their neat shoes
'—and you're wearing sensible shoes. Come along.'

He swept her out of the house and down the drive,
into the lane, and turned away from the village towards
the lake.

After a few minutes he asked, 'What's the matter,
Mary?'

'Nothing—nothing at all. It's lovely here; you have
no idea how much we're enjoying ourselves, and your
mother is so kind.'

'Don't waste time waffling. I asked you what was the
matter.'

'If you don't mind I don't want to talk about it.'

'I do mind. What did Ilsa say to upset you?'

'Nothing—nothing at all...'

'Very well, and now tell me what she said.'

'Don't you bully me,' said Mary crossly. 'You've been
very kind to us, and I'm grateful, but I wish we'd never
come. You've helped us enough.' Her voice rose to a
wail. 'I want to go home.'

'If you won't tell me I'll have to guess. Ilsa told you
that she was going to marry, probably gave you some
proof of it, perhaps told you that she was going to meet
me. Am I right?'

Mary nodded, not looking at him.

'She may even have hinted delicately that I was aware
of your feelings towards me and was concerned
about them.'

'She told you...?'

'I haven't seen her, but I've known her for some years. You're a goose. My dearest girl. Don't you know when a man's in love with you?'

She said sharply. 'How could I possibly? I'm a thorn in your——'

He stopped walking and swung her round to face him. 'Did I say that? I must have been mad. But I'll say this, and you had better believe me. I love you, Mary; I want you for my wife. I think I have been in love with you for weeks.'

'Oh, have you? Have you really? But you're going to marry Ilsa. She said so; she said you were going to be married quite soon and she showed me her engagement ring.'

'Exactly what did she say? Can you remember?'

'Oh, yes. She said that you and she are going to be married shortly; she said she knew where you were. She said... The rest doesn't matter.'

'She was quite right in a way. She is going to be married shortly, but not to me. The ring she showed you wasn't mine, my darling; she's to marry a middle-aged tycoon with a great deal of money who lives in Florida.' He tightened his arms around her. 'So that takes care of Ilsa.'

'Yes, well,' said Mary, wriggling in his arms.

He held her fast. 'Shall we discuss us? Our future—our glorious future together. But you haven't told me that you will marry me yet, my darling.'

'Oh, I will, I will. Isn't it funny that we didn't like each other very much to start with? Well, I thought you looked nice...'

'And I thought you were the most beautiful girl in the world.'

'Really?'

'Really. Now stand still; I'm going to kiss you.'

Mary, a sensible girl, knew when to do what she was told!

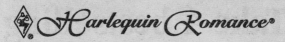

Harlequin Romance®

**brings you another chance to enjoy
one of our most successful miniseries,
featuring kids of all shapes and sizes!**

**Join us as we celebrate the joy,
wonder and humor that children can
bring to any relationship...**

Coming February 1998
McTAVISH AND TWINS (#3494) by Trisha David

Mike McTavish was convinced Erin was a gold digger—
until he saw the tender way she handled his orphaned
twin niece and nephew. But he already had a fiancée....
Could he back out of the engagement honorably, or
would he have to watch Erin walk away from him—and
from the twins?

*Kids & Kisses—
Where kids and kisses go hand in hand!*

Available wherever Harlequin books are sold.

Take 4 bestselling love stories FREE

Plus get a FREE surprise gift!

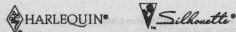 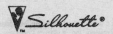

**Make a Valentine's date
for the premiere of**

◆ HARLEQUIN® **Movies**

starting February 14, 1998 with

Debbie Macomber's

This Matter of

Marriage

on **themovie channel**

Just tune in to **The Movie Channel** the **second Saturday night** of every month at 9:00 p.m. EST to join us, and be swept away by the sheer thrill of romance brought to life. Watch for details of upcoming movies—in books, in your television viewing guide and in stores.

If you are not currently a subscriber to The Movie Channel, simply call your local cable or satellite provider for more details. Call today, and don't miss out on the romance!

themovie channel tmc
*100% pure movies.
100% pure fun.*

◆ HARLEQUIN®
® *Makes any time special.™*

An Alliance Production   HMBPA298

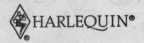
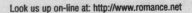